The Forty-Third War

The Forty-Third War

Louise Moeri

Houghton Mifflin Company
Boston 1989

Library of Congress Cataloging-in-Publication Data

Moeri, Louise.
The forty-third war / Louise Moeri.
p. cm.
Summary: Twelve-year-old Uno is conscripted into the army of a revolutionary force in a Central American country that is fighting for its freedom.
ISBN 0-395-50215-2
[1. War — Fiction. 2. Central America — Fiction.] I. Title.
PZ7.M7214Fo 1989 89-31178
[Fic] — dc19 CIP
AC

Printed in the United States of America

P 10 9 8 7 6 5 4 3 2 1

To all children everywhere trapped in war

The Forty-Third War

DAY ONE

"Soldiers. Why are they here so early?" Uno Ramírez's eyes opened at the same instant he heard the heavy trucks roll into the village square. Waking up fast, like a bird that hears a cat, he rolled over, dropped out of his hammock, and let his thin blanket slide to the dirt floor. The others – his mother, the two babies, his fourteen-year-old sister, Concepción – were still asleep; he could see them huddled on their pallets in the gray light of the tropical dawn. Good – he always liked to see what was happening before his mother and the other kids started a lot of noise.

Now he heard it again – the ragged drone of engines as the trucks climbed the low slope that led up from the river. They must have come off the main road that led to the docks on the estuary where the ships were loaded with bananas. And leaving the paved road meant they had some special reason for coming to the village.

It wasn't unusual for soldiers to come – the village expected them like bad weather or sickness. In fact, they were showing up oftener and oftener this year. Uno had already seen bands of them twice since Easter and watched hungrily as they loaded their trucks with melons, chickens, corn. But usually the soldiers didn't come this early in the morning. These troops must have been traveling all night to have arrived here at dawn. Why?

He looked back over his shoulder again. His mother was still asleep on her pallet, where she and the two babies slept since his father was killed, and Concepción was just opening her eyes. He had to move fast. He had slept in his pants; all he had to do was grab his shirt and put it on as he slipped to the door. He was sorry that Concepción was awake but determined to get outside before she could start crying and clinging to him. Concepción was frightened of anyone, certainly of soldiers, and he had to move fast or she would be grabbing for his hand, begging him to keep her safe.

As if anyone could do that, he told himself as he stole out the door. Then he forgot about Concepción as he quickly turned to his right and melted into the shadows of the poinsettias that grew beside the house. From there he could see into the village square without being seen.

Two gray-green trucks had rolled to a halt just inside the square, and several uniformed men had climbed down. They were now clustered close to the trucks.

Not many villagers were out yet. Uno thought those few looked as if they had waked up fast, the way he had, and hurried out to see what was happening. He could see the mayor, old Señor Calderon, who was so crippled from a fall that he walked nearly bent double, and two other old men who worked at the fruit-packing shed. And — yes — there was Uno's best friend, Lolo Sandoval, bobbing around right at the mayor's elbow. Trust Lolo to have his nose into whatever was going on whether it was any of his business or not, instead of staying hidden in the shadows, the way Uno was doing, till he could tell whether it was safe. Uno had learned – the hard way – to be cautious, but Lolo had to poke his nose in and find out about everything. Lolo always knew who was sick or in trouble, how to eavesdrop on the people who went to confession when the priest came to the village, and it was Lolo who long ago learned how to tell the soldiers of the revolution from the loyalist soldiers of the presidente. Both kinds of soldiers came through the village often, but it was Lolo who had figured out that the soldiers of the revolution had better guns – from China or the USSR – but shabbier uniforms than the loyalists. The loyalists had gray uniforms and the revolutionaries green, and there were some differences as to cap and insignia. Uno had learned to identify them too, after Lolo pointed out that the revolutionaries had pictures of a streak of lightning hitting a rock and the loyalists had orange patches with a picture of a bird riding on a dolphin. He could see now, squinting carefully through the pointed leaves of the poinsettia, that these men were soldiers of the revolution.

The two trucks had stopped in front of the mayor's house, partly cutting off Uno's view of the mayor and Lolo, but Uno knew Lolo would see and hear everything and tell him all about it later. Though, of course, there wouldn't be much time. As soon as the whistle blew down at the loading dock he and Lolo and all the other boys would have to leave for work. Thinking of the long, hot day to come as they loaded bananas onto the Norwegian ship anchored there, Uno was almost sorry he was twelve years old and too old to go to school anymore. Anything – even reading and arithmetic – was better than heaving stalks of bananas onto his shoulder all day.

As the minutes passed, Uno waited in the shadows for Lolo to circle around behind the trucks so they could leave for the dock. No matter what was happening, they would still have to go to work. Usually they walked down together with Ignacio, Uno's cousin, who was fifteen, and several other younger boys. Since all of the able-bodied men had been drafted by one army or the other and were gone from the fields and the village, there were only boys and very old men left to work in the fields and at the packing sheds, and anybody who was late for work got his pay docked.

Uno squinted his eyes as the first rays of sun came through the trees. A few more people had arrived, but only the soldiers seemed to be doing something. They were taking some things out of one of their trucks and arranging them – a desk, a couple of chairs, some clipboards and sheaves of papers –

Suddenly Uno realized why the soldiers had come – he turned to run –

And plowed full force into a soldier who had circled around the houses and come up behind him.

Uno lunged back, kicked, tore at the hands that gripped him. But even as he fought he knew it was useless.

No one ever escaped.

Half an hour had passed.

There were still not many people in the square. Old Señor Calderon was still there, standing behind an officer who was sitting at the desk and a couple of other very old men, one of whom, Rodrigo Valdez, was his cousin Ignacio's grandfather.

Uno, his arm clamped by the hand of the soldier who had captured him, was between Lolo and Ignacio. He couldn't move.

The women of the village, including Uno's mother – but not his sister, of course – had come out of the houses to stand in tense, silent clusters here and there. From time to time one of them said something to one of the soldiers, but the soldiers paid no attention. The soldiers were in a kind of ragged ring around the square, and everybody, both soldiers and civilians, were facing the officer, who was now looking at some papers. Lolo and Ignacio each had a soldier gripping his arm.

Uno stared around him. His heart was pounding, and his breath came in uneven, shallow gasps. Although he stood absolutely still, he could feel waves of fear – but mostly rage – rock through him. It was like the feeling you get in an earthquake, and he knew he might not have been able to run even if the soldier had let go of him. But it didn't matter. Running was the worst thing to do. The soldiers always shot you if you ran. If you didn't run, there was a chance you might live.

Uno turned to his left. Lolo stood there, shaking, too. Sweat was trickling down between his eyes. Lolo didn't turn, but Uno knew he was aware of his look. They had been friends so long each of them always knew what the other was thinking. And both of them were thinking, *"Don't run –"*

Uno and Lolo had grown up as if they belonged to the same family and had been together so long they could read each other's minds. Uno could not remember a time when Lolo was not there, within arm's length, as they splashed in mud holes, chased chickens, poked and stabbed each other with sticks, played "baseball" with a stick and a ball made of twine. When they were very little boys, they had given each other nicknames — Pablo somehow became "Uno" and Manolo was "Lolo." As soon as they were old enough they had gone to school — only two years — and then they were taken to the cane fields to help with farm work and to the loading docks when their fathers and the other grown men "disappeared," were drafted, or died. By the time they were nine years old they could talk across a room or a packing shed or the deck of a ship with only an eyebrow twitched or a change of the mouth. Left eyebrow raised meant "look out"; right eyebrow raised meant "all clear." They used their left eyebrows so much both of them developed a permanent upward slant on that part of the face. By now, at twelve years old, they sometimes had trouble remembering which of them had said or done something. Not that it mattered . . .

Uno knew, without even glancing at Lolo, that Lolo was now thinking, "Three men here guarding us. A lot more in a ring around the square. They look tired, hungry. Some are wounded. They need recruits bad. They came before and took the others. This time they take us."

Uno turned a fraction of an inch to look at his cousin Ignacio. Nacio was standing to his left, tall as a man, though still slender, and stooped already from loading bananas. Ignacio did not seem to be angry. But then Uno knew Ignacio had expected this to happen for a long time — it was considered the wildest of good luck that he had never been in the village when the soldiers came. Until now . . .

In some ways, Uno thought, it was almost worse for Ignacio to be caught by the soldiers than for himself or Lolo, because he was the only child left in his family. His mother, who was Uno's mother's older sister, had been the village schoolteacher and his father had been a doctor before both of them had been arrested two years ago for supporting the labor unions.

Since his parents had disappeared, Ignacio had lived with his grandparents, but he had had more education than most, and he continued to read whatever he could find in the way of newspapers and books and talked to everyone who knew something about the outside world. Ignacio also talked about trying to make his way to the capital to search for his parents, though everyone knew this was useless. Señor and Señora Valdez had been arrested by the loyalists, who said the peasants didn't need labor unions, and being "arrested" meant they would never be seen again. No one "arrested" by the loyalists ever returned to his family, and no information about anyone ever came back. Unmarked graves were scattered over the whole country, and farmers were used to turning up bones – if not bodies – in their fields. It was understood, though not talked about, that this was how those "arrested" were "tried." Even though Ignacio never admitted that his parents were surely dead by now, Uno was sure that he knew it.

Uno found himself thinking hard about all these things because it helped to stop the shaking and kept him from hearing his mother. She was standing near the officer's desk, crying, and as she stood there, her hands gripped and tore at themselves like wild animals in a cage. Her mouth was a gaping black hole of grief. "No – no – no –" she kept saying. "Not my son – not my son –"

The officer at the desk rose to his feet. He was tall and thin for a Central American, and his face as he stared around the square was very grave. He was dressed in the same rumpled olive drab uniform the soldiers wore, with a captain's insignia clipped casually to his open collar. He had a gun strapped in a holster at his side and a rifle propped against the desk. "*Silencio*," he said.

Some kind of quiet descended. Señora Ramírez was still weeping, but she pressed her hands against her mouth to stifle the sound.

If I could go to her, Uno said to himself, I'd tell her, "Be quiet! Maybe I can get away – escape –"

"I wish to thank you, *compadres*, for gathering together here so that I may speak to you." The captain paused to look around the square. Uno looked too. What the captain called a "gathering" looked more like people herded into a prison compound. Soldiers stood guard everywhere. Anyone who had not "gathered" here would be shot if the soldiers found him.

The captain went on. "I am Captain Mendoza of the revolutionary army. It is my duty to address you today on the subject of the revolution. Our nation suffers from poverty, disease, illiteracy, oppression. At last we – the common people – have banded together to rid ourselves of a government that oppresses and starves us. We intend to take possession of our own country, our own lives. This will not be easy. But, as you know, our brave freedom fighters of the revolution have made many advances and now have the loyalist dogs in retreat.

Our next big task is to capture the city of San Ildefonso, which will give us control of the northern half of the country. It has been a long struggle, but when our army enters the capital and takes over the presidential palace, we shall free our country from the vicious oppressors who have sucked our blood for so long —"

Uno had a brief vision of the face of Julio Dominguez, the presidente, which he had seen on a poster fastened to one of the loyalist trucks. The presidente didn't look like a bloodsucker. He looked like a fat man who ate often, slept well, and didn't load bananas.

"It is therefore my duty to inform you that the army of the revolution hereby conscripts for active service the following men: Ignacio Valdez, Manolo Sandoval" — that was Lolo — "and Pablo Ramírez."

And that's me, Uno thought.

Three women screamed out loud. Everyone else was silent. Some of the quiet ones had sons too, but they happened to have wakened early today and by now were far back into the jungle.

Uno stared at the ground between his feet. He wished he had waked up early too.

They sat in the shade of the truck for nearly an hour. There had been a lot of talking, and some of the women had gone so far as to attempt to strike or claw the captain. Señora Ramírez had been one of these, and she now sat on the ground in the middle of the square, her face bleeding from where a soldier had hit her. One of her friends, María Chavez, stood beside her. From time to time María surreptitiously wiped the blood from Uno's mother's face and quietly tried to get the older woman to get up and go back to her house. Señora Ramírez would not move, but at least she was no longer screaming at the soldiers.

Uno watched his mother and did not allow himself for one second to glance toward his house. He hoped that Concepción had had wits enough left to hide herself and the babies. Concepción was as likely to stand and scream as she was to hide – since the day some loyalist soldiers grabbed her and kept her in their truck for an hour she had never been a sane, whole person. But whatever Concepción was doing now, Uno was not conscious of any flicker of movement from his house. Even the door had swung half open, stuck in the mud, with only a couple of chickens pecking around.

He decided not to think about his mother and sister, because if he did he might reveal by some passing expression that someone was hiding, and he had a sense that the soldiers were preparing to leave. The sooner they got out of the village, the less damage would be done.

He knew, of course, that when the soldiers left, he and Ignacio and Lolo would go with them. The captain had taken out a pen and filled out some official-looking papers, handing one to each boy's mother. One of them accepted the paper silently as if dumb and blind and the other as if it were a snake or carrion. Señora Ramírez had dropped hers, and María now held it. Uno could hear that paper crackle a little as María moved to cover his mother behind her skirts.

Uno hoped that María could get his mother back into the house soon. His mother had become so enraged when the soldiers did – that thing – to his sister that she had even tried to kill one of them with a machete. They were loyalists, those soldiers, and it was only because there was suddenly word of the approach of a band of revolutionaries and they had to leave at once that they did not shoot Señora Ramírez then.

If she had tried to kill a revolutionary soldier she would have been arrested, tried, and then shot. That was the main difference between the loyalists and the revolutionaries, as far as Uno could tell. The revolutionaries didn't "disappear" you or kill you immediately, but they would conscript you, and you died fighting. The loyalists either conscripted you and you died fighting, or they "arrested" you and you disappeared. Either way you died.

Both sides sent committees of people to the villages from time to time to make speeches about their causes and tack up posters which people immediately took down to use for paper to write on. Uno and most of the others never listened to the speeches, even though they were compelled to stand there, and most of them couldn't read the posters. Both Ignacio and his grandfather could read – Uno could read a little – but no one wanted to know what the posters said anyway. Who cared if the loyalists said they had opened ten new schools this year and were going to hold elections next year – or the year after – if you were dying of malaria this week? In any case, Uno knew he had to load fruit or cut cane to earn money for food for his family, so the loyalists could have opened a school next door, and it wouldn't have mattered to him. Food, on the other hand, mattered a great deal. Right now he was very hungry . . .

Uno jerked his attention back to the present and the soldiers. They had loaded the desk and chair and other things onto one truck, along with some bananas, some tortillas they took from one of the houses, and several chickens whose feet they tied together with string.

Captain Mendoza stood talking to Señor Calderon, and Uno could just barely hear his voice. "Yes, Señor Calderon, it is a great sacrifice. Not one single family in the nation has escaped without making a sacrifice. But it is only with our heart's blood that we will win our freedom –"

"But"– the old man's voice was only a reedy whisper – "will there be anyone left to accept that freedom – to build upon it? I only ask, my captain –"

Captain Mendoza was silent for several seconds. Then he turned suddenly to the men: "*Apúrense!* Load up! *Adelante!*"

Freedom, hell, raged Uno as the soldier beside him booted him up into the truck – they take us prisoner and call it fighting for freedom – ?

The truck with the new conscripts was second in line. It followed behind the captain's truck, its motor grinding and growling and sending back a stink of gasoline fumes to the men riding in the open bed. Where the road was dry the tires threw up clouds of dust that choked them. Where it dipped into the ravines and swamps the truck wallowed in the mud.

Uno sat with his teeth clenched and his hands balled into fists as he watched the road unwind behind the truck. He was so full of rage he felt he would explode. Now, after all these months, he understood how Concepción had felt and why she had never recovered after the soldiers got her. Even though these men had barely touched him, he knew now what it meant to become a prisoner. I will get away, he told himself. They can't keep me. They can't make a soldier out of me.

But there were some orders he had to take, along with Lolo and Ignacio. Several times the trucks got stuck, and all the men were ordered out to push, and Uno wondered then why he had ever thought loading bananas was hard. Lolo and Ignacio were tall enough to push, but the truck was too high for him to get a grip on the tailgate and his feet slid out from under him in the mud. But he pushed anyway, because he knew he had better work up a sweat or one of the soldiers was likely to crack him on the rear with his gun butt.

Around noon they halted. The soldiers climbed out to stretch their legs, and the boys were allowed to step briefly into the bushes, one at a time, under guard, and then told to wait near the truck.

Now the three of them stood in a tight, hard knot, staring at the jungle on either side of the road and at the circle of soldiers who surrounded them like a wall of knives. One man in particular seemed to have been ordered to watch them, and though his manner was relaxed, Uno saw that the muzzle of his rifle followed them like a compass needle.

They knew better than to talk out loud, but Uno had to say one word – the word that had been burning inside his mind since they left the village. Now, barely breathing it out, he said, "Escape?"

Neither Lolo nor Ignacio moved or answered. Their guard,

who hadn't heard Uno, shifted his gun long enough to spit in the dirt and then it swung back to point directly at the center of Uno's back.

Lolo's eyes flickered up briefly. "River." He mouthed the word, not even letting himself give it as much breath as Uno had. He didn't need to. All three of them knew that the road the trucks were following had not crossed the Rio Santa María. That meant that the Santa María lay somewhere to their right, though hidden in the jungle, and if they could get to it, it would lead them back to their village. But without anyone saying it, all three understood that such a journey could easily cost them their lives and that only after they escaped the soldiers – which was clearly impossible at the outset.

Ignacio shook his head, a faint jiggle that could have been the motion to shake off a fly. But he made himself clearer by raising his foot and just by accident bringing the toe of his sandal down on top of Uno's foot. *Stay. Don't run. If we run, they'll shoot us*, Uno read. He nodded slightly.

They stood silent and motionless then, as Captain Mendoza climbed out of his truck and came back to talk to the sergeant who appeared to be in charge of the second truck.

"All right, Díaz, you take the recruits and go on in. You know what to do."

The sergeant nodded. He was short and heavy-set, with a belly that hung a little over his belt. He looked as if he might have black blood in him.

"I will rejoin you before sundown," said the captain. "See how much training you can accomplish this afternoon –" He turned, and he and the sergeant stared at the three boys beside the truck. "I will hold you personally responsible, Díaz, and I expect a good job. If there are any 'injuries' "– the captain gave the sergeant a long hard look – "I will hold you responsible for that also."

Then the captain turned back and climbed into the lead truck. Half of the soldiers climbed into it also, and, as the truck drove away, Uno saw that they had two machine guns mounted and manned in the truck bed and all of the soldiers carried their rifles at the ready.

At the fork in the road the captain's truck turned and disappeared down the overgrown track to the left. The sergeant turned to the remaining men. "Load up!" he barked sharply. Uno and the other two scrambled up into the truck bed, followed by the soldiers, and crouched down next to the chickens, who squawked fitfully and thrashed their legs. Uno felt like one of the chickens, even though his legs weren't tied.

Although the new recruits sat on the floor of the truck bed, there were rough benches along each side where the regular soldiers sat just high enough so they could see out over the sides. Two men rode standing up and facing forward over the cab. Their personal guard still watched them, but all the men had their rifles at hand, and all seemed to have an animal alertness that told Uno they would react in an instant, in case anyone tried to dive out of the truck into the jungle. He could almost feel the burn of a bullet in his back . . .

As the truck coughed and choked and they began to roll forward, taking the right fork in the road, Uno began to wonder what would happen if he asked a question.

"Where – where are we going?"

No one glanced at him or answered.

He waited a while and then tried again. "Where are we going?"

One soldier turned and stared at him indifferently for a moment. Uno tried to catch his eye, but the man looked away.

Uno let several moments pass and finally, as the truck jolted over deeper and deeper potholes and ruts, he said, to no one in particular, "Hey, *compadres* – where are we going?" He tried to look neutral and not like somebody who has just been kidnapped.

The man sitting directly opposite him glanced down. He had a scar from temple to chin. He smiled faintly. "*Compadre?*" he said softly.

Immediately Uno saw he had made a mistake, had overstepped a dangerous boundary. He hoped it didn't blow up in his face. "No," he said hastily, staring hard at the scar. "*You* are the *compadres. We* are –"

"Nothing."

"Yes. Nothing," Uno agreed. It was certainly true. Anyone could see that. He and Lolo and Ignacio – certainly they were nothing. Pigs would have been of greater value than they were at this moment. Pigs could at least be eaten. Uno said no more but rode staring past the soldiers at the rising slopes and the jungle as it thinned to the pine and oak forest of higher altitudes. And finally, after a couple of hours had passed, he recognized that, although they were nothing – not even pigs – they were being taken into the mountains. And that meant they were being taken to the hidden stronghold of the revolution . . .

Uno rode silently now, penned inside himself with his own thoughts. He was angry, he would always be angry. He would always watch for a way to escape. But even as he thought of it, he knew escape was impossible. He could not think of a single man he had ever heard of who had escaped once either the loyalists or the revolutionaries "drafted" him. So . . . it all came down to this. He, Uno, was about to become a soldier.

There were a very few things he knew about soldiers. They marched, fought, killed people, and sometimes – not often – they were allowed to come home between battles. Occasionally they sent messages, pictures, money. And if he, Uno, became a soldier, and stayed alive, he might see his family again. Once in a great while, if there were an earthquake or a volcanic eruption, the soldiers were sent home briefly to help dig out and rebuild. But they never came home because the war was over, because it was never over. It had never started. There was just war, all the time.

Before his father had been "recruited" by the revolutionaries and died in some battle somewhere, he had told Uno that the loyalists wanted to keep the country as it had always been – with a few families owning the *fincas*, the cane and banana and coffee plantations, the packing sheds, with the people working when they could, starving when they couldn't. He admitted that the great families had built some schools, opened some clinics, and maybe a few of the peasants were better off. But the progress, such as it was, was very slow, and, in the meantime, men had to work at starvation wages picking coffee or cutting bananas or sugar cane.

But the revolutionaries, his father told him, wanted to change everything. They wanted the great plantations cut up into small holdings, so the people could have land of their own to live on to raise crops to feed their families. The revolutionaries wanted money removed from the banks to build hospitals, colleges, roads, village schools. And they were willing to fight a war to accomplish all this.

The trouble with that was that in order to win the war, people had to die. And besides that – news traveled, even through trackless jungle – they heard that in the two provinces the revolutionaries now controlled, the people who were left there were still starving, and faster, because so many fields and villages had been destroyed by either one army or the other.

Uno hadn't tried to decide which side was better – loyalists or revolutionaries. As far as he was concerned, he couldn't see that it mattered. Nothing changed much, whichever army controlled your village.

But for now, he reminded himself, he might as well stop thinking about which army was right. Now he was one of them – one of the soldiers of the revolution.

But it was a strange feeling. He had been watching soldiers all his life. Sometimes they were loyalists in light gray uniforms with orange and white shoulder patches that showed a great bird on the back of a dolphin. Sometimes they were revolutionaries and wore dull green uniforms, mismatched pants and shirts, and any kind of hat or cap they could find. They had no shoulder patches but wore shirts with a lightning bolt painted on the backs. Both loyalists and revolutionaries came to the village to "enlist volunteers" and "accept donations" of food and money. None of the "volunteers" or "donations" went or were given willingly by the villagers.

There were times when one army or the other brought a military band to play marches and folk songs during a visit.

Uno and his friends might have enjoyed the music, but they chose to melt back into the jungle instead of joining the dance . . .

Whichever army happened to be there brought men who stood up and gave speeches. Loyalist speakers talked about the new schools and how many people could now read. Revolutionaries talked about how they would cut taxes when they took over the government. Loyalists talked about free vaccinations for children. Revolutionaries talked about how the children who were vaccinated against smallpox later died of starvation or diarrhea. The loyalists sent teachers into the villages to teach many people to read, whereupon the revolutionaries printed and distributed an underground newspaper telling how the presidente, Julio Dominguez, spent $3 million renovating his palace, and his wife bought a pearl necklace for $500,000.

The worst part about it all, his father had told him, was that *both* sides were right. The loyalists *had* built schools and hospitals and vaccinated babies against disease. And the revolutionaries *were* right when they said Presidente and Señora Dominguez rode in a Rolls-Royce limousine over streets in the capital that the city could not fix, past pigs wallowing in the plaza, to dance at someone's palace to the music of a band that cost more than a new water purification system for a jungle town would have cost.

The struggle between the two kinds of people had been going on for all of Uno's life. His father had told him that it had gone on for all of *his* life. Maybe, Uno thought, it had also gone on for all of his father's father's life.

The only thing to do, Uno thought as the truck slowed to

a crawl in a swampy stretch of road, was to try to stay alive. He was not at all sure he could do this, and what it would be worth if he did, but nevertheless, he would try . . .

As the truck toiled up the steep, crooked road gouged into the flank of the mountain, Uno thought they must be nearing the stronghold. The presence of such a fortress somewhere in the mountains toward the northern border of the country had long been whispered about, though no one, of course, knew where it was. Now Uno began to see small groups of men with machine guns just visible on points overlooking the road, and several times he heard sentries shout a warning, and the truck slowed down but did not stop.

At last they slowed to a crawl. The road ahead made a sharp turn and then was barred by a set of heavy post and wire gates set into a high wire fence. There were guard towers on each side of the gate and more towers at intervals in the fence, which stretched away on both sides to disappear in the pine forest.

Uno stared hard at Lolo and his lips formed the words, "Fortress," but he made no sound. Lolo nodded ever so slightly.

Uno took a quick look around. He could see that the fortress was located on an isolated ridge on sloping ground studded with patches of pine trees and was high enough to show a view of mountains on all sides. Far to the south, the direction from which they had come, the icy cone of Atlacatl, the volcano, thrust up like the tip of a knife from the lower mountains. To the north, east, and west were more green folds of forest-clad mountains.

There was a sudden grabbing of brakes and the truck stopped. Now a soldier came forward and the sergeant and driver were identified, then the sentries came around to the back of the truck to look at the rest of the men very carefully. One sentry stood guard while the other climbed into the truck and searched it with a thoroughness that surprised Uno. Not an inch of the truck nor of them was left unexamined.

At last the gates were opened, the driver shifted gears, and the truck rolled into the fortress. Seconds later the gates were closed and the sentries were at their posts again.

Uno sneaked a quick look out through the side rails of the truck. They had come to a halt beside a row of canvas tents. Soldiers were everywhere, more trucks scattered here and there, some large guns he could not identify, piles of some kind of crates under black plastic sheets. Two jeeps sat nose to nose under a tree.

The sound of the truck's motor died, and Uno, Lolo, and Ignacio sat frozen. Then the scar-faced soldier motioned them to dismount.

As his feet hit the ground, Uno was conscious that several soldiers around the compound turned to stare at the newcomers. Some seemed faintly curious, some contemptuous, but most appeared only to have focused on moving objects and immediately looked away.

The three boys remained near the back of the truck. All of them were trying to see as much as they could as fast as they could. Uno now saw long rows of oil drums behind the tents and one large water tank with a dripping faucet. Some distance from the entrance gate a sheet of black plastic had been hung from a clump of trees to afford shade, and under it stood a crude sheet-metal stove and a couple of tables where men were working. A lot of soldiers looked no older than themselves, although they wore uniforms and carried rifles.

Uno wanted urgently to talk to these boys. They were like him – thin faces, spindly legs and arms, hungry-looking. Their uniforms hung slack on them, and their eyes had a curious, blank stare. It was the same blank stare he and Lolo and Ignacio used in the packing shed when the foreman and the bosses were around. But he thought if he could get a chance to talk to one of these boys without the sergeant or the officers nearby he might be able to learn something. He would ask about the food, ask which officer was to be feared, ask if anyone ever got to go home. He would not ask about the war. He already knew about that.

Behind him the truck door slammed shut and almost immediately the sergeant appeared.

"You –" said Díaz, and poked the barrel of his rifle out like a cattle prod. "You – over there." He herded them toward the nearest of the tents, a long, low construction of canvas and wooden boards. "Stop. Stand here." The sergeant stuck his head in at the door of the tent. "Sergeant Batista. Out here." He stepped back as an older man emerged. "Three recruits," said Sergeant Díaz. He and Sergeant Batista turned to look at the boys.

"God," said Batista. "How old are they?"

"Same as the others," said Díaz. "It's all we can find."

Batista stared bleakly at the boys. They stared silently back.

So this is the army of the revolution, Uno told himself. And we're part of it.

*

It was now well past noon, and none of the boys had had anything to eat since the night before. Uno wasn't used to eating much at any time, nor were the others, but they usually had some cold tortillas or fruit to eat in the morning, and coffee now and then, with a little sugar.

Uno was so hungry now that he was beginning to sweat and his knees were weak. As they stood in front of the tent, waiting for whatever was to happen next, he realized that he didn't care what they told him to do as long as he got some food soon. Sergeant Batista had vanished into the shack after ordering them to wait where they were, and they could hear him knocking things around inside and swearing at somebody. Uno was trying to decide how dangerous it would be to ask for food, when Sergeant Batista suddenly reappeared.

In his arms he carried a bundle of the faded and ragged mottled green uniforms the other soldiers wore. He threw the uniforms down on the ground. "Here," he said crisply, "get these on. Quickly. *Quickly*."

They fell on the pile of uniforms like thieves. Jerking and snatching, each of them found a pair of pants, but there was only one shirt. It fit Ignacio and he got it, but Uno and Lolo had to keep their own shirts on. All of the pants were much too big. Uno had seen immediately that the uniforms were made for men and that the other boys who were already uniformed all looked the way he did — the crotch hung inches too long, the legs had to be folded up, and the pants would have fallen off if each of the boys had not been given a length of cotton rope for a belt.

It didn't take long for them to make the change. Their own clothes were gathered up, and one of the boy-soldiers carried them back into the tent. Uno wondered why they kept them — none of the items were much more than rags. Maybe they could find a chance to talk to one of the other boys later. There were a lot of things Uno wanted to know.

They heard the sound of footsteps behind them and a crisp command. "Attention!" It was Sergeant Díaz.

They stumbled around, struggling to straighten themselves into some kind of erect, soldierlike posture. Uno knew, as the others also knew, that even though he was burning to escape, the first need was to survive. And that meant being a soldier, whether he wanted to or not. Tomorrow, the next day, every day, he would watch for a chance to get away. In the meantime, he had to deal with Sergeant Díaz.

Díaz surveyed them and shook his head. Then he said, "You are now privileged to become soldiers of the revolution. Raise your right hands. Do you swear to defend God, your country, and the revolutionary army with all your strength, your will, and your life? Sí? *Sí?*"

They nodded hastily, mumbling "*Sí!*" Uno wondered what might have happened if they had said, "No," but he figured the army was like the packing shed. You could speak up any time, as long as all you said was, "Yes, sir!"

The sergeant nodded shortly. "Now you must learn about your rifle. You will learn to dismantle it and clean and reassemble it — in the dark as well as in daylight. You will learn to shoot to kill. You will learn guerrilla tactics. You will become tigers in your hearts and you will never cease to struggle for the victory of the revolution. But first you can eat."

As one, Uno and Lolo plunged forward. Instantly the sergeant lashed out with his rifle barrel. "Halt!"

Uno and Lolo – but not Ignacio – caught blows in the stomach, face, and chest before they could catch themselves. Bleeding from a cut lip, Uno realized that Ignacio had expected this and had had sense enough not to bolt. He resolved to watch Ignacio and move only when he did. Ignacio knew a great deal about important things.

"Now. That is better," said the sergeant as they stood still. "All right – march. In a line. Over there." He pointed them toward the area where the stove and tables were and jabbed the first one in line – it was Lolo – in the rear. Lolo stumbled into motion and the other two quickly followed, trying to keep the line straight and their backs upright.

"Ah, see," said the sergeant, "how quickly you improve. You will make fine soldiers."

Guided by the sergeant's rifle barrel they funneled into a line of men shuffling past a table made of boards laid across tree stumps. As each one reached the table he was handed a spoon and a tin plate of food and a cup.

Uno's eyes raked across his plate. Beans and tortillas! *And* coffee in the tin mug. He held his plate and cup close to his chest as if afraid someone would steal them.

Through the line the three boys stopped and huddled together. Already accustomed to being herded they froze, waiting for the sergeant to direct them. The sergeant flicked a glance at them and then nodded at a tree several yards away where three other boys already sat eating. They bolted across to the tree and threw themselves down on the ground. Uno grabbed his spoon and rammed beans into his mouth, stuffed pieces of tortilla in, and swallowed so fast his throat hurt. Only when his stomach began to fill did he slow down. Finally, when his plate was empty, he turned to his coffee. He drank it slowly, savoring each brown drop as it slid past his tongue.

When all his food and coffee were gone, Uno set the spoon and cup into the plate and sank back, feeling for the first time he could recall what it was like to have enough to eat to fill him up.

Most of the others were finished too, he saw, including the three boys who had been sitting under the tree when they arrived.

Uno wondered if it would be safe to ask some questions now. Carefully, quietly, he leaned toward the boy nearest to him. "What's your name?"

The boy's eyes flickered at Uno, but mostly he watched the sergeant. "Esteban Morales. Don't talk too loud."

Uno glanced back at the sergeant, who appeared to be busy talking to several of the other men, and all of them were attending to some kind of a paper – it looked like a map – spread on the ground between them. They seemed to be arguing.

Uno leaned forward again, and, speaking just above a whisper, said, "How long have you been here?"

"At the fortress? Three months. Longest I have been in any camp."

Uno searched Esteban's face. It was blank; it neither welcomed nor threatened. He wondered if his own face looked that way to others. "Do you have a family?"

"I have – had – two older brothers. Gone. Killed – a loyalist raid. My mother – I don't know where she is."

"And your father?"

The faintest shadow of something passed over Esteban's face, so quickly Uno was not sure he really saw it. "My father," said Esteban quietly, "was . . . recruited. By the loyalists." Slowly and carefully he raised his coffee cup to his mouth. Uno saw that his hand shook, but again it was only a flicker.

"Loyalists?" Uno said suddenly. "But you are – we are –"

"Revolutionaries. Yes."

In the silence that fell Uno slid back from Esteban, in line again with Ignacio and Lolo, as if it were safer to distance himself from the pain Esteban must feel. "Did you – tell them? The officers?"

"Oh, no. If I had told them my father was a loyalist – or at least fighting for them – they would have shot me."

"Why?"

"They would have known I was a bad risk. A bad soldier."

"But you can't – nobody could –"

"Fight against his father?"

Uno nodded. He felt rather than saw Ignacio and Lolo as they too nodded.

"Well, for a while I just . . . aimed at soldiers my own age. Or officers. Not anybody who might have been . . . my father's age. But it doesn't matter now. He's dead. He was killed in the last big battle. But the revolutionaries – Captain Mendoza – they never knew about it." Esteban raised his cup and drank the last of his coffee. Then his eyes met Uno's like two flat black stones flung out in anger. "And if you tell them," he said softly, "I will kill you. Because I am here to fight for the revolution."

*

Two or three minutes passed, and Uno realized Esteban would not say anything more right now. In any case, he had told them all they needed to know, and that was that they must not trust him with either their confidences or their friendship – certainly not their friendship.

While he was sitting in silence, watching Esteban, Uno caught a movement to his right. Two soldiers had brought a large basket and placed it on the ground near them. Instantly all the men around them rose and hurried over to put their plates, cups, and spoons into the basket. Uno, Ignacio, and Lolo followed.

When the basket had been carried away, the soldiers all relaxed, drifted back into the sketchy shelter of the trees, and dropped to the ground. Many lay back and went to sleep, some sat talking quietly.

Lolo, who seemed to be restless, glanced at Uno, nodded slightly, and wandered off. Uno knew that he was off to find out what he could about their new prison. Uno and Ignacio went back to the place where they had eaten and sat down. Ignacio lay back and closed his eyes, but Uno sat up, silently cataloging everything he could see.

First off, he wondered if he could make a good guess at how many men were in the fortress. Counting the thirty-odd men who had come with them in the trucks, and those sentries outside and inside, plus those he could now see, he figured there were at least two hundred, maybe more. But even two hundred did not seem like a very large force with which to fight a war. Especially when some of them – himself, Lolo, and Ignacio, and probably many others – were recruits barely a few hours into the army. When I went to bed last night, he thought, I was a twelve-year-old kid working in a packing shed loading bananas. Today I'm a twelve-year-old soldier, but I still don't know anything except how to load bananas. I sure hope we manage to get out of here before we have to fight any battles.

"Where's Lolo?" muttered Ignacio.

"Looking around. He'll be back," said Uno. "If he doesn't get into trouble snooping around . . ." And only because he knew how Lolo did it, Uno was able to tell that he had managed to see a lot of the camp by the time he returned a few minutes later.

"It's bigger than I thought," said Lolo quietly as he sank down beside Uno and Ignacio. "But if we could get over the fence —"

"Probably guarded —" said Uno.

"*Sure* guarded," said Lolo.

"Of course. So that's out. And the gate is guarded too. But trucks go in and out," suggested Ignacio.

They considered this. Some of the trucks were open flatbeds, some had side rails, a few were covered with tarpaulins.

As they were looking at the trucks, the boy who was sitting next to Esteban spoke. "No. You are not going to escape — desert, I mean. Not now. Not ever. They search all the trucks before they go out. Or come in."

"Come in? Why do they search the trucks when they come in?" asked Uno, remembering that the truck in which they had arrived had indeed been searched. "Why would anybody want to break *in*?"

"To blow us up. Loyalists."

"Oh." Uno nodded glumly. Lolo looked disappointed.

Ignacio sat up and leaned forward. "What is your name? Are you a . . . recruit?"

The soldier – a boy of maybe fourteen – sat up stiffly. "I am Juan Cardoza. I'm not a *chiclero* or a *cortero.* I was in school. I quit to become a soldier. I'm going to help win the revolution."

Uno stared at him. He could not believe that anyone really wanted to fight in this war. Or any war. So long as he could remember he and his family, his friends, the people of his village had had one single common cause – to escape joining either the loyalists or the revolutionaries. No amount of leaflets, speeches, or slogans from either side had ever persuaded them that death was preferable to life, that killing people was better work than loading bananas or cutting cane in the fields. And certainly nothing had persuaded them that war was going to make life better for them in any way. "*Why?*"

As Uno's question hung in the air, they saw a ripple of movement spread through the camp. Juan squinted at the officers, who had rolled up their map and were getting ready to move off. "They will start training you now. Yes – I want to serve the revolution. I want to throw those rich landowners and foreign bloodsuckers out. We will win – and we will have a people's government – elections – freedom – peace –"

They were all on their feet now, and Uno and the others were careful to do quickly and exactly what everyone else did. The boy-soldiers headed for the tent where the uniforms had been handed out, and they followed. Uno hoped they were going in the right direction. He didn't want to be a soldier, but he had sense enough to know that from now on the only choice left to him was to be a soldier – and a good one, if he could. There didn't appear to be any way out of the fortress, and he had a fair idea that Sergeant Díaz had ways of making life very painful for one who didn't learn to be a good soldier . . . quickly.

"Peace?" whispered Ignacio as they hurried along. "When was there ever any peace? This country has had forty-two revolutions since 1900. *They* were all going to bring freedom and peace too. They never did. What makes you think this one will be any different?"

Now the sergeant was coming at them like a tank. With the barrel of his rifle he quickly sorted them out, sending the experienced men to the left and the new recruits to the right. As Juan turned left, Uno saw him cast one last shocked look at Ignacio. Juan's lips moved silently. *"Forty-two?"*

"Forty-two." The number sank into Uno's mind like a rock thrown into a pool of water. Forty-two wars had been fought, and he was now here with his friends preparing to become soldiers in war number 43. He wondered briefly if the forty-third war might be any different from those that had preceded it and finally decided that if it were, it was only because they would be carrying guns instead of running from them.

Sergeant Díaz had a way of telling them to do things, as he lined them up, that was like a new language, and Uno realized immediately that the language was something he should have learned last year. Díaz directed them with both the barrel and butt of his rifle, but no matter how quickly Uno followed the gestures, he could not get where he was supposed to be fast enough. Why doesn't he *show* us what to do? he raged silently, as the sergeant's gun butt cracked his rear for the third time.

But now he saw that the new recruits had been formed into a line opposite a shorter line of experienced soldiers. Then the newcomers were fitted into the other line so that each recruit was between two trained men. Or rather boys. But the boys, never mind their age, seemed to understand the sergeant's signals. They managed to march, wheel, lunge, drop to the ground with no more than a second's delay from command to execution. The sergeant did not bother to explain his directions – all hand signals now – but as he stumbled forward Uno began to sort them out and name them. There were Forward, Halt, Ground, Left, Right, Aim, Fire.

The soldier in front of Uno was a lanky boy of about fifteen whose face was marred by a cleft lip. He said nothing at all to anyone as he flawlessly executed maneuver after maneuver, and Uno wondered how long it had taken him to become so expert. While Uno stumbled and groped for directions and grunted curses, the only sounds the other soldier made were the thump of his boots on the ground and the whistle of his breath through his deformed mouth. Uno began to think of him as the "Whistler," as he struggled to follow his lead.

The afternoon wore on, through what in happier times and better places might have been siesta, and the heat increased and the dust clogged their noses. Sweat poured down under his loose uniform, and soon everything Uno had on was wet. The wetness actually helped, because as the sweat evaporated it gave a faint sense of cooling to his hot skin.

After what seemed forever but probably was only two or three hours, the sergeant halted them down-slope from the main buildings of the camp. When his signal came, Uno did not see it because sweat was streaming into his eyes. He crashed full force into Whistler.

Instantly Whistler whirled on him and raised a hand for a karate chop at Uno's throat.

"Stop!" The sergeant's voice raked down the narrow line like a whip. "We kill the enemy. Not each other."

Shakily Uno reached up and wiped his eyes clear. When he could see again he was looking into Whistler's eyes. They were slanted, a kind of catlike gold brown, and Uno immediately understood that Whistler was fully as dangerous to the men and boys around him as he was to the enemy.

Next was a short rest period during which they were dismissed and allowed to throw themselves down in the shade. Sergeant Díaz went off a few paces and stood talking to some other men, also sergeants. A messenger was sent back to the Headquarters tent, and presently they saw three men hurrying toward them with plastic jugs and tin cups. They scrambled to their feet, quickly formed a ragged line, and grabbed the cups of water as they were offered. The water tasted warm and had a chemical smell, but Uno gulped his down as if he had had nothing to drink since yesterday. Then the three water carriers gathered their jugs and cups and returned to the tent.

Uno went back to his shady spot and lay down. Lolo sat

down on one side of him and Ignacio on the other.

Uno stared up at the sky. It was a clear burning blue laced over with the sharp needles of the pine tree under which they rested. It reminded him of times at home in the village, times when they had stopped work for a moment, to look around, to look up at the sky –

"My God," said Uno suddenly, "we've only been gone a day. Less than a day. It seems like forever."

Lolo nodded.

"It is forever," said Ignacio softly. "None of us will ever go back."

They were silent for several moments. Then Uno said, "My mother . . . my sister . . . the babies. What will happen to them now that I'm not there? I was the only one left to work in the packing shed. My mother can't work – she has to take care of the babies. And my sister . . ." His voice trailed off.

Neither Lolo nor Ignacio spoke.

Then Juan, who was sitting only a few feet away, said, "The army will take care of them. The revolutionists have a committee that goes around and brings food and clothes to the families of the soldiers."

He seemed confident as he spoke, but Lolo gave him a long, hard look. "My father was taken to fight for the revolutionaries two years ago. How come we never got any food or clothes? These –" he glanced down at his mismatched uniform – "these are the best clothes I ever had – and they probably came off a dead man."

"So does everything that the revolutionaries give out," said Juan bluntly. "Where else would they get anything?

When people get killed or houses – a village – gets bombed or burned, they go in and take whatever they can find that's left and give it to the people who are still alive. Dead people can't wear a shirt or eat beans."

Ignacio looked at Juan thoughtfully. "All the same, nobody in our village was ever given anything. We lost plenty – both the loyalists and revolutionaries used to take food – beans and rice and chickens and eggs and fruit – but we were never given anything."

Juan shrugged. "So? No system is perfect. But it will work out in time. When we win the war –"

"The forty-third war –" put in Uno.

"When we win, we will have a free government, and jobs, and doctors, and –"

"The only thing any of us is ever going to get out of this war is the ditch they throw us in when we get killed," said Ignacio bleakly.

"*Atención! Atención!* Fall in! You will now receive your rifles!"

"See?" said Juan as they scrambled to their feet. "And you said the revolutionary army wouldn't give you anything!"

Uno figured it must be nearing five o'clock in the afternoon as they again assembled by the main tent. There were several tents – seven or eight in all – stretching right and left in a ragged row across this upper level of the camp, but as far as he could see, most events of importance happened at this one. The only thing that set it off in any way was the small wooden table that sat in front of it. The table was scarred, the legs uneven, and the brown paint was worn through on the top. Uno thought it looked like the same table that Captain Mendoza had used that morning in the village. The presence of the table here gave him an ominous, uneasy feeling, as if he was always going to be standing in front of some battered table while the man behind it disposed of his life.

Then, while Uno was still trying to get his chin back and his legs straight, the flap of the tent popped open and Captain Mendoza emerged and seated himself behind the table. Immediately three or four other officers appeared out of nowhere to stand on either side of the captain.

Uno was a little surprised to see the captain. They had seen him climb into one of the trucks and drive away when they were on the road to the fortress this morning, and since then so much had happened that the captain had simply ceased to exist for him. It was like watching a kind of magic act now to see him arrange some papers on the table and then come around to the front of it to stand facing them.

"*Atención!*" bawled a sergeant.

They snapped into positions something like that of real soldiers.

"I see you have already begun your training." The captain's voice was not loud, but it had a curious, carrying quality, and he seemed to be speaking to each man individually. "Sergeant Díaz has given me a good report of your drill this afternoon. He tells me that you new recruits are learning fast." He paused and this time his eyes coasted carefully over Uno, Lolo, Ignacio, and some others. Uno made sure his face was blank and his eyes never left those of the captain. It was impossible to believe that Sergeant Díaz could have said anything favorable about them, but maybe tomorrow a miracle would happen and some of them would learn the difference between the commands and which feet were left and right.

The captain went on. "It is my greatest regret that we can allow you so little time in which to be trained. But we are – after all – revolutionaries. That means that in order to begin our struggle for the freedom of our country, and then to win that struggle, we have to assemble an army and train it under the most adverse conditions. We do not have large bases and unlimited equipment or plenty of time to practice maneuvers. We have to hide in the jungle, accept harsh living conditions, and make use of the most basic tools. Today Sergeant Díaz has been teaching you how to fight a guerrilla war by using silent hand signals. He tells me that you have done well. Tonight"– he paused and again his eyes raked across their faces – "tonight you will be issued your guns."

The captain fell silent. The old soldiers were silent too and unmoving, but all at once Uno felt his belly turn cold and sweat break out across his shoulders. A *gun?* Somebody is going to hand *me* a *gun?* Holy Mother of God – I only just learned to cut cane with a machete without chopping my foot off a couple of years ago. I can't even use a slingshot or throw stones and hit anything – I'm a *kid* – a *kid* – a dumb *kid* –

"We understand –" The captain spoke again, and his voice suddenly seemed somewhat ragged, as if he were hoarse from a bad cold or from talking too much. "We understand –"

Again his eyes looked into them, although this time Uno was conscious of some kind of curtain that seemed suddenly to have fallen between the officer and the soldiers. "We understand how difficult it is for you to learn so much in so short a time. Some of you have done very well. Some are a bit slower. Those of you who have had some training must therefore devote every moment you can find to teaching all you know to the new men. Practice the moves. Rehearse the signals. When you receive your guns, practice loading and unloading the magazines, aiming, carrying. You will be issued your rifles and receive a demonstration now. Without ammunition, of course. Only the experienced men carry ammunition. You will keep your rifle with you tonight, until drill is finished. By tomorrow I expect you to know how to load and unload it in the dark without making any noise."

He paused for a moment as Sergeant Díaz approached, handed some papers to the captain, and then fell back to stand behind him. In that moment Uno turned with a startled look at Lolo. "They're going to give us guns?" he whispered. "How do they know we won't –"

But Lolo signaled "*shut up,*" and just beyond Lolo, like a black moon coming up, Uno saw Juan leaning ever so slightly forward to look at him.

That's how, he thought.

The fact of the matter, of course, was that the more experienced soldiers had already long since been issued their guns and had been trained to use them. This was clear to Uno as he watched them now file into the tent on the left and emerge carrying rifles. Juan and Esteban carried their weapons as if the steel sprouted from the palms of their hands; there was a polish to their movements, almost a grace, as they lined up again.

Sergeant Díaz signaled to the new recruits. "Forward." His eyes bored into their faces. "After me." He led the way into the arms tent.

Inside it was much darker, and Uno could barely see. There was some kind of counter or table and behind it stacked wooden crates or boxes. Two or three men in officer's uniforms were behind the table, and they turned as the new boys gathered before them.

Díaz grunted, "Ramírez."

Uno stepped forward. An officer behind the table leaned over and picked up something from a box on the floor.

Uno stared at the rifle that was being held out to him.

"Take it!"

His hands came up like wooden levers, and he felt the weight of the rifle fall into them. He managed to close his fingers in time so he didn't drop it. Dazed, he fell back into line and stood staring down at it. It was the strangest-looking gun he had ever seen. It looked like the skeleton of a gun – a short barrel with a raised sight, a grooved case underneath that curved forward, a metal hand grip, a leather sling with buckles, and a stock that was only a metal shaft with something shaped like a tiny steel foot at the end. There were levers and knobs he didn't recognize.

"That is an AK-47," said Sergeant Díaz. "We captured a

shipment of arms last month, but we do not have enough ammunition for them. You new ones will use them because you don't know how to shoot anyway."

Uno stared at the sergeant but said nothing. After a moment he let the mouth of the rifle barrel tilt downward. If the thing went off somehow, he thought, at least it wouldn't kill anybody. Then, inside himself, he heard a voice say, "But that's what it's for . . . killing somebody . . ."

One by one the others received their rifles. All of them were AK-47s, like Uno's, but some of them had different stocks. Different too were the boys' ways of accepting and holding them. Ignacio took his as if he had been handling guns all his life – he hadn't – but Lolo acted awkward and clumsy, and Uno knew he had not only handled guns before, but had even fired them. His father had been a rather successful bandit before the revolutionaries had conscripted him. Some of the other boys seemed excited, looking down at their rifles as if at an interesting new toy.

"Shoulder arms – like this," said Sergeant Díaz impatiently. "Return to the line."

All of the new recruits turned, utterly forgetting what little they had learned about marching and immediately clashed into a tangled mass with rifle barrels whacking and clattering. Uno got a sharp crack on the butt from Lolo's gun as Lolo swung in a half circle trying to get his rifle free so he could balance it against his shoulder. Uno had his gun partway up to his shoulder when the curved piece of the stock caught on his shirt and pulled it up to his armpits.

"God in heaven!" bawled Sergeant Díaz. "I'm to fight a war

with *this?*" He ripped Uno's gun out of his hands, freed his shirt, and jammed the rifle into place against his right shoulder. The others fumbled into position. "Out! To the line!" They scrambled through the tent flap, which hit Uno in the face, and back to their places in line.

"Thank God they don't have any ammunition," muttered Juan. Uno fell in between him and Esteban.

"Pigs," said Esteban.

They drilled until darkness came. There were several commands covering the handling of the rifles: Shoulder arms. Present arms. Ready, Aim, Fire. At ease. The movements were simple, but the weight of the rifles immediately made their arms ache. Uno wondered if any of them would have strength enough to hold his weapon up, aim, and fire with any accuracy, assuming they lasted long enough to even get into a battle. But he watched Juan, Esteban, and Whistler closely and before long could produce a rough copy of the movements, though none of it made any sense. If you were going to shoot somebody, you couldn't expect him to stand there while you shouldered arms, marched forward, dropped to one knee, and then took aim and fired.

Just before full dark, Sergeant Díaz dismissed some of them and marched the rest downhill to where patches of forest covered the flanks of the mountain, almost out of sight of the tents. He lined them up – Uno and the other new recruits and an equal number of somewhat more experienced boys.

"We will have an exercise now to see how much we have

learned. That little rise there"— Sergeant Díaz gestured at a nearby bare knob – "is held by the enemy. We will advance through the trees – silently – to the bottom of the rise, creep up the slope, and then rush the crest and capture it. Keep your weapons up out of the dirt and make no noise. Esteban, take these five men. Juan, take the rest. Now –" He nodded toward the shadowy hill.

Uno, Lolo, and three others fell to Juan's band. They turned and followed him as he angled sharply to the left. Juan ran lightly, making so little noise Uno felt his feet didn't even strike the ground. Juan held his rifle close, and his back was bent so that he was crouched to take shelter behind the scant cover of bushes.

At the bottom of the little slope Juan paused. With gestures of hand, fingers, gun, he separated his group of five across perhaps twenty feet of space, but where all of them could still see him. Lolo fell over a tree root and Uno squatted down too close to a bush and hooked the barrel of his rifle in its branches. When Juan's signal, a sharp hiss, came to move forward, both Uno and Lolo were late. In the gathering darkness Uno immediately realized he had lost his bearings too, but he knew if he didn't keep up with the others he would certainly take a blow from Sergeant Díaz. Yanking his rifle free of the bush he plunged forward and crashed full into Juan's back. By the time he had scrambled out of the way, recovered his sense of where objects were in the dark, and plunged forward again, he heard cheers break out above them. The other group, led by Esteban, had "captured" the hill.

Juan stood up, spitting curses. "You filthy stinking pigs!"

he hissed. "You couldn't find up from down! Can't you see – are you blind? Idiots? God – what kind of war can we fight with pigs like *this?*"

Uno and Lolo drifted closer to the other recruits as Juan turned on his heel and led the way back toward Sergeant Díaz. They fell in line behind the sergeant, sullenly aware of the air of triumph of Esteban's recruits. The winners said nothing, but the faintest shades of movement told it all, in the way they walked and carried their guns, the way they took the lead in the straggling column, shouldering the losers to the rear.

Uno glared at their backs as they tramped back up the hill. He was filled with a smoking rage. He didn't like being a loser. He hadn't asked for this damn job, but he didn't want to be a loser, stuck at the tail end of the line, laughed at. Dammit, he raged silently, I didn't want to be a soldier, but I damn sure don't want those bastards to beat me at it. I don't want anybody to beat me at anything. "I think we just lost the battle," he grunted to Lolo, who was just ahead of him.

"Battle?" said Lolo grimly as they stumbled through the darkness. "We just lost the war!"

When they returned to the tent area – Uno was beginning to think of it as "Headquarters"– they saw the other men lined up for the evening meal.

Again without thinking, Uno and Lolo lunged forward, only to have Juan stop them in their tracks.

"Hold the line. Now – stack your rifles here – against this

tree. Be sure you can find yours when you come back."

Uno and Lolo placed their rifles side by side. The several guns stacked around the tree made it look like a mangrove tree with air roots. Uno thought he would be able to recognize his because the revolutionary sign, the lightning bolt, was scratched on the hand grip in yellow paint. Then Juan signaled them to join the line where plates of food were being handed out.

Uno was so hungry his hand shook as he took his tin plate, and his coffee slopped a little. Staggering with fatigue and weakness, he made his way to the same spot where they had eaten earlier in the day. Lolo followed, and Ignacio and Esteban.

When the meal was finished, Uno thought their duties for the day would be over also. He was astonished to hear, as the recruits stood in an aimless cluster near the Headquarters tent, that they were to gather for more training.

"Now?" he muttered as Juan signaled them to move toward a clearing near the gun tent.

"Now," said Juan. "Pick up your rifle."

They retrieved their rifles and trudged up the slope toward the clearing, where two small propane lanterns made a pool of light on the trampled ground. Directed by Juan they dropped to sit in no particular order, except that all of them faced the lanterns and Sergeant Díaz, who squatted next to them with a rifle in his hands. Uno could not find a comfortable way to sit holding his rifle and started to lay it on the ground but was stopped by a glare from Juan. "Rifle out of the dirt!"

Díaz rose to his feet. "These are AK-47s which you have been issued," he said. "You will carry these for now. We have very little ammunition for them until the next shipment can be air-lifted in, so there won't be much target practice. AK-47s are automatic weapons. They can fire as many as six hundred rounds in a minute. This is the magazine." Deftly Sergeant Díaz removed the curved metal case that thrust down and forward from the center of the rifle. His hands were broad and blunt and looked clumsy, but Uno could see that he was enormously skillful in handling the rifle. "It is loaded like this – inserted like this. Now – remove your magazines – reload – remove –"

For several minutes they practiced removing the magazines from their rifles and reinserting them. After several blunders and some pinched fingers, they began to do it right. Then Sergeant Díaz took a small handful of bullets out of his pocket, handed exactly one to each recruit, and showed him how to load it. Again the minutes passed as they practiced inserting the single shell into the magazine, removing it, and repeating the move, over and over.

"Now," said the sergeant, "do it with your eyes shut. And don't make a sound."

After half an hour's struggle, the boys could close their eyes, remove the magazine, load the shell, and then reinsert the magazine into the rifles. They had even learned not to drop the shells, rattle the magazines, or crack gun barrels together.

"Slow," grunted Díaz. "Slow. You must learn to move

faster. In a battle –" Suddenly he halted. In the dim light from the lanterns they saw that his attention had suddenly gone away from them. His hand raised for silence. Looking at him, Uno thought his face must look something like that of a jaguar who senses the approach of danger.

Then, in the pause, Uno heard something also – the faintest far-off rumble of some kind of motor.

In the time it took Uno to identify the sound as something other than the wind, or approaching trucks, Sergeant Díaz had snuffed out both lanterns. And suddenly the silence of the night was ripped open by the pulsating roar of big motors close overhead.

"To the trees! To the trees! Raid! Raid!" shouted Díaz. "Run, you bastards! Head for the trees! Take cover!"

In the darkness Uno leaped to his feet. Momentarily blinded, he could see nothing but then felt Lolo grab his arm.

"Over here – run!"

"*Where?*" cried Uno.

"Rocks – trees – run –" Lolo's voice was leading. Without thinking Uno plunged after him.

"Saw – good place – to hide –" panted Lolo as they raced across the uneven ground. "Ignacio – ?"

"Here – here –"

Then Uno felt the ground beneath his feet change; he cracked his shins on stone, found himself on the ground, crouched in the lee of a pile of rocks. Crooked trees sprouting through the boulders sheltered them somewhat from the sky. Near him he sensed other men, heard voices, felt legs, arms, feet around him like tangled snakes.

He had just opened his mouth to ask what they were running from when he realized that it was a sky full of helicopters. Even village boys knew the difference in sound between helicopters and planes. The copters – he could not tell how many – seemed so close overhead he thought they must crash into the side of the mountain.

Then he heard another sound – a steady flat chatter that seemed timed to slashes of light against the black sky. Guns! They were being shot at –

Explosions of white fire lit up the scene and dust swirled up. Uno heard muffled sounds like *ptch! ptch!* and he thought this must be larger shells striking the bare earth. Other sounds were sharp, splintering, and then a whining afterecho – shells striking stone or metal – the trucks?

What he did not hear was the sound of men crying out – screaming –

In the space of a minute – two – three – the raid was over. The copters withdrew down the mountainside, and very soon their roar died away.

As the beat of the rotors died out, Uno felt a faint stir in the darkness around him and then a slow gathering and shuffling. He got to his feet, although he was shaking so bad he could hardly stand. "Lolo," he whispered, "are you all right? Nacio – ?"

One by one a grunt or a curse identified each of the others as still living. Uno was surprised. He had not expected any of them would live through the rain of fire. "Who – ?"

"Loyalists," said Ignacio. "Who else would attack this place? God – why didn't we fight back? Doesn't *this* army have any ships like that?"

From a few feet away Juan's voice said sharply, "We

do. We have several Hueys, same as those. But they're not here. We're too exposed. Too much danger of their being destroyed."

"Too much danger of helicopters being destroyed?" bawled Uno. "How about *us* being destroyed?"

"They can get more soldiers," said Juan calmly. "We're cheap. Copters cost big money. We have to buy Hueys on the black market. General Godoy only uses them when he thinks it's worth the risk. Come on."

They stumbled after Juan, and Uno sensed that other men, perhaps the whole camp, was gathering for something like a roll call.

They clustered in rough groups near the HQ tent, where Captain Mendoza and some other officers were listening to reports on the damages. From the quiet questions and answers, Uno realized that there had been some losses, some casualties. They waited in silence, however, for the captain to speak.

"Five dead," said Captain Mendoza presently. His voice was level, emotionless, controlled and controlling. "Seven wounded. This was a bad hit. Those copters should have been turned back by our other units when they crossed the river. Sergeant Batista, take charge of the wounded men. Sergeant Díaz, take two men and make a complete survey of all damages to the trucks and other equipment. Sergeant Perez, dismiss the rest and see to it they get as much rest as possible."

"Dis – missed!" Sergeant Perez's rough voice was a door slamming between the soldiers and the captain.

Uno watched silently as Captain Mendoza turned and disappeared into the HQ tent, followed by one officer who carried the propane lantern and another who picked up the table and took it inside. Then Uno, Lolo, and Ignacio turned toward each other, and all three of them turned to Juan.

"What – ?" Ignacio began, but was interrupted by Juan.

"Bring your rifles. I'll take you to the supply tent and you will each be given a blanket and a hammock." He started across the clearing.

They jumped to follow him.

"Where will we sleep?" asked Lolo. "In one of the tents?"

Juan snorted. "You? You'll sleep outside like the rest of us. You can string up your hammocks on trees or sleep on the ground. Only the officers sleep in tents."

"But – snakes?"

"Rain?"

"How cold does it get up here?"

Juan dismissed all their worries with a flick of his hand. "Snakes – very few up here. The loyalists will kill you before the snakes do. Rain – it's too early in the year for rain. And you get used to the cold. We are revolutionaries."

As Juan paused in front of a tent down the row, Uno muttered, "How much fighting can we do if we get sick?"

"Don't worry," said Ignacio quietly. "The loyalists will take care of that too. They will kill us before we have time to sneeze."

"Watch out, know-it-all," said Juan as he went into the tent. "You may turn out to be so smart they'll send you out on reconnaisance."

"What's re – con –" asked Uno.

"Never mind," said Ignacio. "I know what it is. It's a quick trip to the cemetery."

*

Juan distributed one blanket and a rope hammock to each recruit and then led them downhill to where a patch of trees offered some thin shelter against the dew and the night wind. Uno made a move toward the rock outcropping where they had taken shelter during the raid, but Juan said bluntly, "That's taken. The rocket experts are up there. They are the most valuable men, next to the officers and the copter pilots, so they sleep in the safest places. You – new, useless – will sleep here, under the trees."

The trees he led them to were hardly more than large bushes, certainly not strong enough to support the rope hammocks. They would have to sleep on the ground, and the ground here sloped sharply. A person sleeping here, Uno saw, would have to be somewhat wakeful so as to keep his head pointed uphill.

"Keep all your clothes and boots on. If there's a heavy dew get closer under the bushes –"

"Scorpions?"

"If you see a scorpion, sting him," said Juan. Then he turned on his heel and vanished into the darkness.

The three boys stood in a huddle. Looking around, they found that two other newcomers, Diego and Manuel, had been directed to this same spot. Uno could vaguely see the blurry shapes of each of the others, hear their faint movements, the sound of their breathing.

"Well, then," said Ignacio, "this is it. Let's try to lie close together. If it gets very cold before morning we can take turns sleeping in the middle. That might help a little."

Slowly, fumbling in the dark, they felt for rocks and sticks (and snakes and scorpions) and gradually prepared a small clear space. One by one they unrolled their blankets and tried out various ways to wrap themselves. Since they were trying to lie close to each other for warmth, this led to cracked heads and some elbows in ribs, but finally they had squirmed into a kind of heap in which each of them was violently uncomfortable but equally unwilling to withdraw and be alone.

They were all exhausted and the younger boys, Diego and Manuel, fell asleep almost instantly.

Uno lay looking up at the sky. "My mother always told me to say my prayers at night," he said quietly. "I wonder if she would want me to do that now."

Ignacio had turned on his side so that his voice was muffled. "Of course. If you can think of anything to thank God for – go right ahead and do it. And you can ask Him to bless Sergeant Díaz – and Juan –"

"– and Whistler," said Uno.

"Whistler?"

"The one with the cleft lip. He almost killed me today." Uno could still see those glaring yellow eyes.

"Oh, by all means. Ask God to bless Whistler. And the soldiers who kept us under guard on the way up here –"

"– and Esteban –" said Lolo.

"Yes," said Ignacio. "He led the team that captured the hill. And if we don't all do better tomorrow he will probably use us for target practice. That should make better soldiers of us."

"If that's what it takes," said Lolo from the far side of the cluster, "we ought to be good soldiers already. The helicopters used us for target practice already."

Uno pushed his feet down and discovered they had thrust out from under the blanket. He drew his legs up again. For a few minutes he lay there, letting the day run through his mind again like a movie. From the moment in the village square when he realized he was in the hands of the revolutionaries, through the day of traveling, eating, drilling, attacking the hill, even through the nightmare of the raid – it all flickered past him once more. He felt as if he had lived a century and traveled a million kilometers since dawn. Worst of all was the knowledge that he, that all of them, had been overpowered, captured, made to be something for someone else's reasons. Well, I may be here, he acknowledged grimly, but I'm not one of them. They can't make a real soldier out of me, even if they do give me a gun. I'll go through the drills because I have to, but I'll wait for a chance to get away. Maybe I'll get out of here. Maybe I won't. But I'll never be a soldier . . .

One day. We have been here, he told himself, for *one day* . . .

DAY TWO

He woke sometime during the night, and for some reason the first thing he thought about was Easter.

As he lay on the hard ground, staring up through the clear air of the highlands at the enormous crystal stars, he remembered the time three years ago when his father had taken them all to church at Easter season.

There was no church in the village, nor even one in the nearest market town, so they had had to walk for more than six days over jungle and mountain roads to the city of San Ildefonso, where there was a beautiful cathedral.

It was Easter of the year before the twin boys had been born, so there were just the four of them to make the pilgrimage – Uno, Concepción (older and quite superior, of course), and their father and mother. Uno had been about nine years old.

They carried mats and blankets to sleep on, and some food and water, and there were many people on the road to talk with, who were also going to San Ildefonso for the Easter observance. Uno's mother, Anna, and his father, Roberto, seemed so much younger and stronger then – he remembered that they sang songs along the way and told stories. His mother's hair was still blue black then, not dried out and gray as it was now, her round face was gentle and loving, and her colored skirts swished around her brown legs as she urged him and Concepción to walk faster.

"Hurry! Hurry!" she cried gaily. "We must get to San Ildefonso in time to see the procession!"

"What is a procession?" Concepción asked.

"A great parade. They will carry statues of Mary and Jesus through the streets and they are so beautiful that your heart will melt when they are carried past you."

"What is a statue?" In those days Concepción liked to keep a conversation going by any means she could find.

"A statue is a thing of great beauty, carved or made somehow out of wood or stone or plaster. It is made in the form of someone whom we must think about. If the statue is of Mary, we must think about how good she was so that God chose her to be the mother of his Son. And if the statue is of Jesus, then we must think about the greatness of God, who sent his Son, and how perfect our Lord was to come and be crucified to redeem us."

"What is 'redeem us'?" asked Concepción again.

"Redeem is —"

And so the days went, and though all of them got tired, it was a wonderful journey. There had been no real outbreaks of the endless revolutions for several months, so the people of the villages had felt fairly safe to make the pilgrimage.

They had arrived at last in San Ildefonso late in the day on Good Friday, camped in the fields outside the city, and on the following day, along with countless others, had packed the streets and the plaza of the city to watch the great procession.

Wonderful and glorious as it was, Uno remembered only bits of the procession. There were musicians, the Bishop, and many priests, and the great statues borne on some kind of wagon decorated with ribbons and flowers and drawn by many men. By the time the procession had come, however, he was tired, his stomach was queasy from all the excitement, and even though his father held him up, he could not see very well.

What he did see, and would remember forever, was when their mother and father took the children to the cathedral that night to see the statue of Christ in Bondage.

The church had been almost dark, and the statue stood where the only light fell over it. It was the size of a real man, standing with head slightly bent and hands clasped before it. The figure was draped in something like white satin, and around the wrists were garlands of paper flowers made to represent bonds. The bonds, like chains, stretched from the figure to a wooden cross behind it. And although the bonds were made of flowers, Uno felt, looking up at the statue, that they must cut that guiltless man like the cruelest steel. Even then, he understood that bonds you didn't deserve were the worst kind. Standing there, he had felt the pain of the imprisoned Christ.

When their parents led the children away, Uno noticed something else. In a small pen next to the statue was a magnificent black and white rooster. His comb and wattles glowed red, and his yellow feet were so clean they looked like yellow gold.

"What is the rooster for?" asked Uno.

"The rooster is there to remind us about Saint Peter. You see, Peter asked Jesus what the disciples could do to save Jesus from the crucifixion. And Jesus told Peter that he had come to be crucified for us. And Jesus told Peter that even he, Peter, would deny knowing Jesus 'before the cock crows thrice.' And Peter did. He was afraid – he failed. But after our Lord was risen, Peter became his great apostle. Every one of us – like Saint Peter – will commit sins and betray those who trust us, and the rooster is there to remind us of that."

"What is an apostle?" asked Concepción.

And so it went. But Uno still remembered the force of the sorrow he had felt at seeing the captive Christ and the strange sickness that crept over him when he thought of the rooster crowing to announce that Saint Peter once, twice, three times denied knowing the Lord. It shouldn't have happened that way, he had thought that day so long ago. Saint Peter and all of them should just have listened to the Lord and done what he told them to do. And why did Peter do such a thing? I wouldn't have betrayed anyone who trusted me, if I'd been there . . .

And then he slept again.

He awoke again before dawn. The sky was still very dark, but in the east the stars had dimmed and on the horizon the volcano, Atlacatl, glowed faintly pink. It was hard to say if it was the first gold of the sun that gleamed on the mountain or the mountain itself. Atlacatl had always been a threat in their lives, along with the overseers at the fruit-packing sheds, and tax collectors, and the soldiers, and sometimes Uno found that he talked (inside himself, of course) to the mountain just as if it were one of those others. "Hey, you, volcano," he would say as he stared at its dagger-sharp cone towering above the jungle. "Hey, you – don't throw fire at us today. My mother is sick – we couldn't run away today." Sometimes he asked the volcano to go ahead and erupt. "Why not today? There are two ships in the harbor to load – I am so tired my legs are breaking. Why can't you blow up today?"

But Atlacatl never listened. He blew up or not, just as he pleased, and, after a while, Uno got to thinking that all the world was pretty much like Atlacatl and blew up or not, just as it pleased, without regard for *campesinos*, or children, or even, maybe, soldiers and armies and presidentes . . .

But now, all at once, he heard the sound of footsteps. He turned over in the tight tangle of arms and legs, and down the slope he saw a man walking. It was the captain.

Uno watched him for a few seconds, then suddenly decided to get up. He did not intend to speak to the captain – it was already clear in his mind that a twelve-year-old soldier who didn't know which end of his rifle the bullets came out of did not approach a captain. In any case, there was nothing for him to say. Yesterday, there in the village square, he might have pleaded, argued, cursed if he'd been given the chance. Today, twenty-four hours later, he knew nothing he could have said would have made any difference then and certainly wouldn't now. And he also knew, in some cloudy, obscure way, that Captain Mendoza had not made the war or made him a soldier. He couldn't tell how he knew this, but it seemed to have something to do with how he remembered those bonds that bound the Christ.

He realized that he couldn't go back to sleep now. He crept out from under the blanket, after moving Lolo's arm from across his chest, and carefully stood up. The others were all still asleep.

Down the slope the captain paused. He stood with his back to Uno, his arms crossed on his chest, and he seemed to be looking at the volcano also.

Uno hitched his pants up and stretched briefly. He was used to sleeping in his clothes, but not on open ground, and he was stiff and chilled. As he moved away from the rest of the boys, his foot came down on a round stone and it rolled out from under him.

The faint noise reached the captain. He whirled suddenly, and his hand flashed to the revolver at his side.

Uno froze. He realized now – too late – that even here in the fortress one must never come up unexpectedly, silently, behind someone. Another man might have shot him where he stood.

Uno forced himself to speak. "Pardon – Captain. Pardon –"

Captain Mendoza stared at him for a second longer, then seemed to consciously signal himself to relax. "Be careful," he said shortly. "Don't be *too* quiet. If you are walking up behind someone – as now – let him know you are there. Or he might just shoot you, because that's what he's trained to do. Shoot."

Uno looked around. It was now light enough to see the

soldiers who slept, or were rising, on all sides. And the guns, the guards at the gate. "Sir – even here?"

The captain smiled grimly. "Especially here. What is your name?"

"Ramírez. Pablo. They call me Uno. I was – I came here yesterday."

The captain had relaxed a little, although his hand still rested on the butt of his revolver. "Ah, yes. You are from the village where we stopped yesterday." He nodded absently. He was already thinking of other things. "Yes, indeed. Ramírez. So, then – carry on –"

"Sir"– and even as he heard his own voice Uno wondered what he was going to say, and where he got the courage –"Sir – am I permitted to ask a question?"

The captain paused. "One question."

"Sir – will we – will this army – win the war?"

For one moment the captain turned away, facing the HQ tent and the day and the duties. Then he turned back to Uno.

"My cousin says – my cousin says there have been forty-two revolutions in our country," said Uno, stumbling to get it out before the captain turned away. "None of those wars helped. This is another. Will the war be won – this time?"

The captain stared at him. The slope was steep here, and Uno was above the officer so that he had a curious feeling of being taller than the captain, although of course he was not. For a moment the captain's eyes were blank and black, like a photograph or a statue. Then something in them shifted, opened or closed, and Uno had one momentary glimpse of something beyond the flat surface. It was terrifying.

"I don't – know," said Captain Mendoza, his voice barely

a whisper. "All I know is — the great need. This country has a volcano for a mother, a jaguar for a father. The children suffer. We must . . . *try*."

Uno went back and sat down near Ignacio and Lolo. The sun would break over the horizon in a very few minutes, and the camp was rapidly coming to life. As he watched, clusters of men were gathering. First they all lined up in front of a screened-off area marked LATRINES on a rough signboard. After leaving the latrines they hurried off in several directions. Some went to where the trucks were parked. Some disappeared into the tent which held the weapons, some went to the shelter where food was prepared. At the farthest edge of the compound two men with shovels started to dig a series of holes.

Uno watched the men with the shovels idly at first. They seemed to be very energetic about their digging, as if it had to be completed quickly. The holes they were making were deep and long and narrow.

Uno suddenly dove at Ignacio, grabbed his arm, and shook him. "Nacio! Nacio! Wake up!"

Ignacio's eyes flew open. "What? Where?"

"Look — look — what they are — what are they doing?" He hauled at Ignacio, and the older boy sat up. Uno pointed down the slope.

Ignacio stared silently. Then, "They are digging graves," he said quietly. "Must be for the men who died in the raid last night."

Suddenly a shrill whistle blasted through the trees. It was

not very loud, but every man in the fortress seemed able to hear it. Those few who were not yet at work now came scurrying out of their makeshift shelters, rolling up blankets and brushing their uniforms. They hurried toward the latrines and then scattered through the compound.

"Up," said Ignacio briskly. He stuck a toe in Lolo's ribs and shook him. "You're not in the village – this is the army. We get to be soldiers again. You, too, Diego, Manuel. Up – up –"

Uno grabbed his blanket and started rolling it. As the others scrambled up, sleepy, grouchy, stumbling, he snapped their blankets up and shook them. "Come on!" He poked Lolo. "Hurry! We'd better get moving before Juan or somebody comes after us. I've been watching – we go down there"– he nodded at the latrines – "and then –"

"And then we find out more about killing people?" groaned Lolo.

"I think," said Uno thoughtfully, "we're going to find out how they bury people here."

But instead of a funeral, the day started with more drill. They were allowed a scant cup of coffee, and then Sergeant Díaz appeared and quickly divided them into groups of ten. Each group had at least one or two experienced men who were given orders by Sergeant Díaz to conduct certain exercises.

Once again Uno, Lolo, and Ignacio found themselves together with Juan and Esteban, but Manuel and Diego and some other new recruits were put into another group with Whistler.

Juan was in charge. He instructed them to address him as

"Corporal." His first order was for them to clean their rifles. They sat on the ground near a pine tree and for nearly an hour practiced taking their rifles apart, cleaning them (after the first time this became simply make-believe), and reassembling them. The final move was to do it all with their eyes shut, which Uno supposed was so they could handle the guns in darkness. Once again, he found himself working to perfect the moves, not because he wanted to clean a rifle, but because it galled him to have other boys do it better.

During the second hour they held "war games." Juan led them to the lowest area of the fortress where the open savanna of the upper regions gave way to the rank jungle growth of a deep ravine that he said was the headwaters of a stream which cut all the way to the coastline, forty miles away. The total area of the ravine included inside the fortress was small, but the jungle was so dense that it might have been many hectares.

Here Juan had them practice moving through the thick undergrowth so as to make the least noise and expose themselves to view as little as possible.

Uno had lived near the jungle all his life, and he thought he knew how to hide in it. Now he learned that he was as awkward as a truck and noisy as a herd of cattle. Juan could slip between two vines without moving a leaf; he could cross the swampy bottom of the ravine leaving almost no trace. His rifle never slipped out of his grasp, he did not lose his direction, and he could count seconds silently and accurately. When Juan sent them on timed forays Uno judged wrongly on both time and distance, got lost, cursed himself, the war, and Juan. Especially Juan.

Beyond the work, it was breathlessly hot in the ravine and very damp. Within a few minutes all of them were panting from exhaustion and soaked with sweat. Black flies bit them, and they had to watch constantly for snakes – bushmasters and fer-de-lance both liked swampy bottoms like this.

Uno knew he was awkward with his gun, so he tried to excel in stealth. He slid under the spreading leaves of a low palmetto and watched his footing so he didn't stumble over the springing roots of a strangler fig tree. In the dim light here on the jungle floor there were many shadows and many shades of green. Vague brown and black shapes high in the trees were spider monkeys intent on feeding. Where there was open water the trees leaned out so far that even here there was little sunlight, although they did catch glimpses of birds, flycatchers, motmots, egrets, that seemed like flashes of light. The smells of rotting vegetation were everywhere, as well as the smell of the slick black mud and even of their own sweat. Uno thought with longing of the cool dry slopes far above them where yesterday they had "attacked" the hill. His belly was empty and he had sweated until he craved water. But still Juan drove them on.

They were threading their way through a patch of bamboo, Lolo just ahead of Uno, when Juan signaled Uno to "attack" Lolo. Uno lunged forward, hooked the barrel of his gun on a liana, and crashed on his face behind Lolo. Before he could roll over and scramble up, Lolo had whirled, dropped astride his body, and raised his rifle as if to crush Uno's skull.

"Good," said Juan from his position a little above them. "Smash his damn head in. He'll never make a soldier. But *you* will."

Slowly Lolo peeled off Uno and they clambered to their feet. Their eyes met in a desolate glance. Uno knew they were once again thinking the same thing: what would have happened if it had been Juan who landed on Uno's back? Juan looked like the kind of soldier who would kill somebody just for practice.

At last Juan directed them back up the ravine, out of the jungle, and on across the flank of the mountain to the little ridge they had practiced on yesterday.

As they made their way up the steep trail, rifles balanced across their shoulders and faces streaming sweat, Uno muttered, "I'd like to kill him. I'd like to kill *him*."

"Juan?" Lolo darted a quick glance back to make sure they were too far from Juan to be overheard. "He's a bastard. But he'll teach us to fight."

"If he doesn't kill us first."

"Shut up." Ignacio was two places back in the line. "You got off lucky, Uno. You didn't pay attention to what you were doing. This isn't the packing shed. This is war. You make a mistake here, they leave your body to rot. Pay attention."

"Listen to the big soldier talk," said Uno sourly.

Ignacio shrugged. "We're here. We've got no choice. We might as well try to stay alive as long as we can."

When they reached the little ridge they were given some water to drink and allowed a minute to catch their breath. Uno stared up the slope. Yesterday he had memorized the position of every tree, every bush, every hump and hollow – even the smell and feel of the dirt. He already knew how many strides, how many lunges, it took to reach the top. He knew how the dry dirt rolled under their feet and how the crest of the hill was like an overhanging lip that seemed to push them back just as they reached it. He wondered if this lesson would go any better than the last one had.

As they squatted in the brush, staring up the slope, Uno turned to see Lolo behind him.

"You think we'll go up a hill when some loyalist is shooting down at us?" Uno whispered.

Lolo looked bleakly back over his shoulder. "You bet we will," he said, "because Juan is going to be behind us – and he'll shoot us if we *don't* go up the hill."

"Would he?"

"Yes, he would."

The bushes parted and Ignacio crawled toward them. "I've got it figured out," he told them as they squatted waiting for Juan's signal. "What we do is – we pray hard for God to save us, and we shoot every loyalist we can see, and we try to stay alive long enough so *we*"– he circled a hand to include the three of them – "can get promoted and be back there where Juan is."

Uno wiped the sweat out of his eyes. "What if God doesn't hear us and we don't hit the loyalists? None of us has even shot one bullet yet."

"I have," said Lolo. "I've shot my father's gun. I like it. Makes a devil of a noise and something falls over. Like a bird or a monkey."

Uno glared at him. "Lolo – we're talking about killing enemy soldiers, and you're talking about killing something so you can eat it. Monkeys don't shoot back at you."

Lolo shrugged. "Gun is a gun," he muttered. "Killing is killing. And I *am*"– he paused, snorted a short laugh, and then went on – "I *am* shooting something for supper. I bet you anything they wouldn't feed us if we got in a battle and made too many mistakes."

"They wouldn't have to," grunted Ignacio. "If you make too many mistakes in a battle, you'll be dead and nobody will need to feed you."

Uno stared up at the gravelly slope. All at once he had a terrible vision. He saw himself – and Lolo and Ignacio – sprawled, dead, on some bleached-out stretch of grass, with bloated, rotting flesh being gouged away by the bloody beaks of vultures.

Suddenly the signal came to attack.

Without a moment's thought Uno rose to his feet, yelling like a howler monkey. He charged up the slope, came down on the defenders like a bolt of lightning, and before they knew what had hit them, he had clubbed their rifles out of their hands and taken them prisoner. They stared at him as if he had dropped out of the sky. Behind him, Lolo, Ignacio, and the rest of the team were only halfway up the slope.

In the stunned silence Juan climbed the steep rise. "Son of a bitch," he said reluctantly as the captured troops "surrendered," "you'll make a soldier yet."

Then he signaled them back down the hill. "Return to camp," he said. "We'll eat. Then we come back here."

"I can hardly wait," whispered Uno as he picked up his rifle and wiped the dust off the barrel. His AK-47 looked as if it had been played with by pigs. "I always wanted to be a soldier."

Esteban, coming up from somewhere, pushed him forward down the slope. "You damn well better," he said. "The loyalists have taken Jacinto Province, and if they capture San Ildefonso, we're going to have to take it back. In a couple of days we won't be playing games here in the fortress. We'll be shooting loyalists. And they will be shooting us."

The sun stood near to noon as they crossed the slope back to HQ. Uno felt his head spin and his knees start to buckle. With nearly hysterical relief he saw the men lining up for food. After stacking their rifles they fell into line and watched with ferocious care as each man moved forward to receive his tin plate, spoon, and cup. Uno thought that the servers might give the younger boys one extra spoon of beans, though he was too hungry to care. The moment his plate was in his hand he started shoveling beans into his mouth. Juan gave him a contemptuous look, but Uno turned his eyes away. Juan had been here long enough to have built up some reserves of fat and muscle; Uno and the others were still at the hunger level that most people in the village lived with daily.

Once again they gathered under the same tree. Juan and Esteban sat near each other and slightly apart. Uno, Lolo, and Ignacio clustered together like family with hands flying to stuff beans and tortillas into their mouths. A brief memory of what Esteban had said about San Ildefonso came back to him, and then he dismissed it as unimportant. Food – that was the important thing.

Suddenly Uno paused. "Meat!" he exclaimed. "There is meat in these beans!"

"Today is Sunday," said Juan. "The meat is an extra gift from the officers because it is Sunday."

"And because somebody stole a cow," added Esteban.

"Like I said – a gift," Juan said calmly. "Eat fast. There will be a funeral now."

Uno glanced up from his nearly empty plate. "I saw them dig the graves this morning. Who . . . died?"

Esteban belched. "Five died last night in the raid. And another . . . a new . . . soldier this morning. He was only here a couple of weeks. Same age as you, Ramírez." He smiled pleasantly.

Uno stared back flatly at Esteban. "His family . . . will they be notified?"

"Of course," said Juan.

"Of course," said Esteban.

"And taken care of, like you said?" pursued Uno.

"Of course," said Juan.

"Of course," said Esteban.

Uno's and Lolo's eyes met. *"Of course,"* they repeated gravely.

The funeral was conducted in the blazing sun. All the men were lined up in a square formation so they made a wall around the open spot at the HQ tent. Here the captain's table had been covered with a length of white cloth, and on it were some candles in tin holders, some sprays of green leaves in empty food tins.

The officers, all in full uniform, stood before the men at measured intervals. Captain Mendoza stood near the table, but he did not look at it.

The ceremony was brief and consisted of short prayers and a simple eulogy, although the officer who conducted the service was not a priest. Watching, Uno remembered other funerals he had seen. When someone died at home, a coffin was made and the body washed and dressed and placed in it. Everyone went to pay his respects, and then when the coffin was carried to the cemetery, they all followed in procession. Flowers were brought, and somebody – a priest or old Señor Calderon – said prayers. Everyone joined in the prayers and laid flowers on the coffin and the grave. And everyone shared the grief. Here, in this army and on this hot, dry mountain, he did not see anyone pray, no one brought flowers, no one appeared to grieve. I don't understand, he thought. They make us be soldiers. Soldiers die. That's what they're for – dying. Doesn't anybody *care?*

When the ceremony was finished, signals were given and the men formed into columns. Sergeant Díaz marched them down the hill to where the six empty graves lay open to the sun and the blank blue sky. Now a separate company of men appeared bearing six stretchers, four men to each stretcher. On each stretcher lay a long, blanket-wrapped bundle.

Uno felt his breath freeze in his chest as the first stretcher bearers passed him. The bundle they carried was almost exactly the length that he himself would have been, if it had been he on the stretcher instead of the dead man.

There was a quick succession of orders, and from somewhere a couple of musical instruments appeared – a trumpet and a flute. Uno listened in silence as the simple clear notes of the national anthem sounded over the graves and echoed upward against the side of the mountain. Then, abruptly, the six bodies were lifted off the stretchers and into the graves.

"Sal – ute!"

Every man snapped a salute. But Uno saw that the men stared straight ahead. None of them watched as men with shovels quickly stepped forward and began to fill in the graves. The loose soil was tramped down hard and smoothed over quickly.

"About – face!" Sergeant Díaz's voice was as unruffled as if he had been ordering them to fall in for rifle drill. "Forward – march!" The column of men marched briskly back up the hill to Headquarters, where they were dismissed.

"A very fine funeral," Uno heard Juan say casually to Esteban as they headed for the trees to escape the sun. "Not everyone gets that much respect."

Uno thought of the silent, blank-faced men, the blanket-wrapped bodies, the falling dirt. "*Respect?*"

Juan nodded. "But of course – the first one . . . he was Captain Mendoza's son –"

For a short period they were free to do whatever they wanted. Juan, Esteban, and most of the other soldiers stayed close to Headquarters, gathered wherever there was shade, to talk, smoke, rest, or sleep.

Uno, Lolo, and Ignacio wandered toward the rocky outcrop where they had sheltered from the helicopter raid the night before. The trees growing among the rocks were small and crooked, but they made patches of shade and up here a light wind blew. The boys settled where they could still see the Headquarters area, though not hear any voices.

Ignacio reached inside his shirt and brought out a few cigarettes. Gravely he gave one to each of the others. Surprised – but grateful – all of them accepted. As Ignacio produced one match, all leaned forward quickly and they managed to get the three cigarettes lighted before it went out.

Uno watched as Ignacio hastily dropped the tiny, curled black fragment of burned match and then covered it with soil.

"Where did you get the cigarettes?" inquired Lolo. "I haven't seen any for a long time."

"Stole them," said Ignacio calmly. "Somebody left a pack in his shirt when he took it off while we were down in that damn ravine this morning." He looked regretful. "I only took three. I was afraid to take any more."

Uno felt a flicker of anxiety. "We'd better be careful. Keep out of sight. If anybody sees us smoking they'll know we stole them."

One by one each smoked and finished his cigarette, then carefully stubbed it out, all except Lolo, who saved a scant inch of his and carefully pinched it out. "I'll finish it tomorrow," he told them.

"Tomorrow," muttered Uno. "If tomorrow is going to be like today, I'd just as soon skip it." He wondered if the others were still thinking about the burial service. Is that the way it all ends? he wondered. We are dragged out here to fight a war nobody ever wins and when we are killed they just dump us into a grave and play one chorus of the national anthem and go out and kill more people. Even Mendoza's son – his own son — did not escape. And without realizing that he spoke aloud he said: "Escape."

Ignacio was sitting where he could see Headquarters and the officers near it. "Put it out of your mind," he said. "There's not going to be any escape. We are here. Same as the ones who were buried today. They didn't get away. There is no way for us to get away. Whatever happens tomorrow, we'll be in the middle of it."

Lolo wrapped a green leaf around his cigarette stub and put it in his pocket. "I wonder how long the war will last."

"Too long." Uno was thinking about Juan, and Whistler, with his venomous eyes. He wondered who he feared more — them or the loyalists.

"Maybe we'll win," said Lolo. "That's something to think about."

"We never have yet," said Ignacio. "And if we did — if the revolutionaries won this time, they would just become the new loyalists — because *they* would be the ones in power. They would elect a president and pass laws, but we — us poor, damn, dumb *paisanos* — will all just go on working and being hungry. Then in a year or two somebody else will start another revolution to overthrow *them*. And either the new revolutionaries, or the loyalists — our own revolutionaries — will need us for soldiers. So we'll be conscripted again, do the fighting. What's the difference?"

Lolo raised up to peer briefly over the rocks. As his eyes swept the pounded earth of the fortress and the scattered groups of men he shrugged. "I'd just as soon be here as back home. There is nothing for us there but to load bananas or cut cane."

"But the bananas don't shoot at you." Uno reminded him.

Lolo shrugged again. "Sure they do. They just don't use a gun. My father was a soldier for a while with the revolutionaries, but he finally deserted – he got away somehow – and came home because he knew we needed money. We were starving. And he went back to robbing people – yes, he did – because he couldn't make enough money at the packing shed to take my baby sister to the doctor. When he finally stole some money it was too late. My parents took her to the doctor at San Ildefonso, and the doctor said if they had brought her a few days earlier he might have saved her. She had measles. So the bananas killed my sister. They killed my father, too. He finally got caught robbing a store, and the police shot him right there. He stole three pesos and a can of tomatoes."

"But the store owner needed his three pesos. And his tomatoes," said Ignacio grudgingly. "He probably had a family to feed too."

Lolo smiled. "Well, he may have got his tomatoes back. But for sure the policeman kept the three pesos."

All of them were silent, remembering Lolo's father.

Then Ignacio said slowly, "My mother was a schoolteacher. She said if the government would educate everyone – the peasants too – then things would be better."

"The policemen are educated."

Nacio frowned. "No – something more than that. She didn't mean just that kind of education. She wanted people to have more than just reading and writing. And mathematics."

"I can do mathematics," said Uno. "One peasant plus one Russian rifle equals one revolutionary soldier."

"Sure," said Lolo. "And one plate of beans and tortillas

plus one peasant plus one rifle equals one very *mean* revolutionary soldier!"

"Well – I have the beans and the rifle. Now, if I could send a sack of tortillas home to my grandparents I guess it wouldn't matter so much – being here. I could fight in anybody's army," said Ignacio. "Like I said – loyalist or revolutionary, it makes no difference to us. All we do is fight. And die."

Uno stared up at the sky fringed with pine needles. "This morning I saw Captain Mendoza. I asked him –"

"You *what?*" Ignacio looked shocked.

"I asked him if we would win the war."

Even Lolo's blank face was surprised. "You spoke to the captain? You can't do that! Even *I* know that!"

"Well . . . I did." Uno hunched his shoulders defensively. "He was just standing there. I guess he was . . . thinking about his son."

All of them were silent for a moment, remembering the ceremony, the marching, the song, the graves.

"Well . . . so what did he say?" asked Ignacio.

"He said we had to win it. He said the country has a great need. He said the country is like . . . like a family of children with a volcano for a mother and a jaguar for a father. He said we had to fight – to win the war . . . because the children suffer."

"Volcano or jaguar or snake bite or break your leg – what difference does war ever make? Nothing changes – ever – for us," said Lolo. "The rich men – they get richer and they get fatter. We get skinnier and we die."

"Captain Mendoza isn't fat," said Uno.

They were silent for a moment. "Well," said Ignacio, "there

are a few – some revolutionaries, maybe even some loyalists – who really mean to make things better. The trouble is – none of *them* ever gets elected president."

"What about Mendoza?" asked Uno. And even as he said it, he wondered what there was about Mendoza that seemed to set him apart from the other revolutionaries. Even Sergeant Díaz treated him with a grudging respect.

"Mendoza?" said Lolo indifferently. "*He's* the one brought us here."

"If he hadn't, someone else would have," said Ignacio. "We would all have been conscripted sooner or later. Everybody is. But . . . yes . . . Mendoza is a good man, I believe."

They were silent for a while.

"He looks like a good man," said Lolo reluctantly at last.

"One way to find out," said Uno.

"How is that?"

"Elect him president – after we win the war –"

The whistle blew, and as they scrambled up Uno listened to the echo of his own words inside his head. That's funny, he thought. Why did I say that? I've never even thought about elections or presidents. And Mendoza *is* the one who came and took us from our homes. All the same – if I had to vote for a president, I would vote for him. But, of course, I won't ever vote for anybody because the war will last forever.

Drill went on till it was too dark to see. They practiced moving through the jungle, rehearsed all the hand signals, and finally spent an hour learning hand-to-hand combat. All of them were natural fighters – there wasn't much in the villages for boys to do to amuse themselves, except to wrestle – but now they began to learn some new moves. Juan and Esteban, naturally, were already experienced (and gifted devils, to begin with), and they threw themselves enthusiastically into making Uno, Lolo, and Ignacio wish they had never been born. After an hour of having his feet jerked out from under him, his head cracked on the hard ground, and his arms almost unhooked at the shoulder, Uno became profoundly grateful that he was a soldier. There was just an outside chance that, given a couple of bullets for his rifle, he might be able to kill either Juan or Esteban – or both of them – under the general cover of the war. When the session ended the three boys staggered away wordlessly and rolled themselves up like bruised worms inside their blankets.

DAY THREE

The whistle seemed to blow even earlier this morning. It was the third day, counting the day they were "recruited," and Uno opened his eyes smelling the cool dry air and the pine trees of the mountains instead of the jungle, as he would have done in the village.

As he uncoiled his arms and legs from the thin folds of the blanket and cautiously tried out stiff joints and back, he remembered what mornings had been like at home: his mother rustling around to make some coffee and find him a tortilla to eat before he went to the packing shed, his baby brothers pulling at him and babbling baby sounds. And Concepción lying blank-eyed and silent on her pallet while everyone else, it seemed, went on living without her. Concepción seemed to have stopped living since that day . . .

Funny, thought Uno suddenly. I had got so I hardly noticed Concepción when I was there at home. Now – here – miles away and a soldier in the army of the revolution, I can see her as if she were right here in front of me. He thought about her long dark hair, uncut and mostly uncombed, and her thin cotton dress, her bony legs and arms like dry sticks, her face, pretty, but with something gone out of it, like an animal beaten too many times. Long ago she had been talkative and busy, but now she only whispered to herself, or cried for someone to keep her from getting hurt.

But we couldn't keep her from being hurt that time when the loyalists came, he told himself, as around him the others crept out of their blankets and pulled themselves together, and no one can keep her safe now. When . . . *it* . . . happened to her, people in the village said she should be taken to a doctor, a hospital. But we had no money for a thing like that. So the loyalists just smashed her, and nothing was done to punish them. I wish I could talk to Captain Mendoza about this. I guess he'd say that things like what happened to Concepción are the reason why we are fighting the revolution.

But what I don't understand is – how a war is going to make things different. Because right now I know that Concepción and my mother and the babies won't even have enough to eat without me there to work in the packing sheds. Juan says the people we left behind will be fed. That's a lot of bull. Nobody *ever* brought anything to us – all they did was take food away.

They were given hot coffee with sugar, and then Díaz assembled them into squads for drill. Once again, Uno, Lolo, and Ignacio fell to Juan's squad, and Juan the Merciless pounded them up hill and down, hour after hour, till their heads ached and their legs wobbled.

At noon they were dismissed and staggered back to Headquarters for a meal of beans, rice, and tortillas. They ate all they were given, and Uno unashamedly licked his plate of bean juice and picked up his crumbs from the ground. Two grains of rice had stuck to Lolo's chin, and Uno scooped them off and ate them too.

After the meal they rested for a while. Their rifles were stacked against the trunk of a pine tree, and they flung themselves down in the shade of another, aching, exhausted, blank, and mindless. They slept for perhaps an hour.

When he awoke, Uno thought for one terrible moment that it was morning again and that he had another whole day to go through.

Then he heard a strange sound. It was a smart, sudden *thwack!* followed by the sound of running feet. He rolled over and opened his eyes.

Across the compound, not far, in fact, from the burial ground, several groups of men – mostly enlisted men but a few officers too – were playing baseball.

Baseball! Uno exploded to his feet. "Lolo! Nacio! Move! Look – baseball!" His toe cracked each of them in the ribs. "Wake up! Look!"

Lolo and Ignacio rolled to their feet wide awake. "Who's pitching?"

"Where'd they get a – God in heaven – what a catch! He's out – no – he's safe!"

The three of them crashed through the ring of spectators to line up at the batter's left, eyes riveted on the pitcher, the catcher, on Esteban, who was up at bat.

Instantly they were surrounded by those spectators they had cut off and were thrust back to the rear. They leaped up, dodged, lunged sideways to see as Esteban swung – missed – was out.

"Out!" bawled Uno. He hated Esteban anyway.

Esteban glared around him as he threw the bat down and stomped off to the sidelines.

The bat was grabbed up by Whistler. Uno ground his teeth. No! That lovely bat – that precious bat he could almost feel clenched in his own fingers – to be in the hands of the yellow-eyed monster!

The pitcher – a man named Cruz – threw the ball. Whistler swung and missed. Uno groaned. *I* could have hit that, he told himself.

Another ball. Whistler missed. Uno wanted to cry. Third ball. Whistler swung – and hit. The ball arced up and into the blue sky, seemed stuck there, and then turned and raced back to earth – solid into the hands of the man on first base. Whistler was out. Uno felt joy all over.

"God," he whispered to Lolo and Ignacio, "I never knew they played baseball here! I'd have joined their damned army years ago – I'd have begged to join it – if I'd known they played baseball!"

They hung around all afternoon, waiting – pleading – demanding – a chance to play. Finally, about four o'clock, the older men and the best players got tired, and the younger boys fell on the bat and ball and mitt like vultures on a carcass.

After a furious struggle, Nacio wound up with the catcher's mitt, Lolo got second base, and Uno, glaring like a wildcat at all around him, got the bat. The pitcher was a short, chunky Indian called Diego.

Uno crouched slightly and flashed back over all the times he had ever managed to hit a ball – even though it had been a stick bat and a ball made of wound-up cord. He knew he was good at it.

Diego wound up like a wooden toy, but he wasn't as dumb and awkward as he looked, Uno quickly found out. The ball sailed past his belt and into Nacio's mitt. It was a little outside.

"Ball!" yelled somebody behind him.

Diego wound up again – it looked as if he would dislocate his arm – and this time the ball was a little lower, but closer in.

"Ball!"

"Shut up!" screamed Uno. "That was no ball – that was –"

"Shut up and play!"

Diego wound up. This one, Uno told himself.

He pivoted slightly, and as the ball left Diego's hand he could see it sailing toward him – his eyes never left it. He felt his arms flow outward and change into the wood of the bat – felt the lovely, lovely *smack!* as the bat hit – and then he threw it down and started to run.

He passed first base, second, couldn't find third – there, there – ran with pounding feet – home – home – a *home run* –

"Ramírez," said Captain Mendoza mildly behind him, "that's the best run I've seen today."

They played till it was too dark to see. Uno scored two more runs, but Diego quickly got his measure and the balls got harder to hit. Diego was squat, silent, built like one of those stone carvings his people used to make out in the jungle, but he seemed to be able to send each pitch just a degree higher or lower than the last one, making Uno sweat with the intensity of his concentration.

Although both Uno and Diego grudgingly allowed others turns at batting and pitching, and though no one would have admitted anyone else's superiority at the cost of his own, Uno knew that he and Diego got to bat and pitch oftener simply because they were the best players. Uno had a strong suspicion he might be better than some of the players on the older team, although he had sense enough not to say so.

When darkness finally fell they had to quit. It was only when they staggered away from the small playing field and back to Headquarters for the evening meal that Uno suddenly remembered that he was a soldier, this was a fortress (a prison, as far as he was concerned), and they were at war. Somehow, it didn't matter so much tonight.

His arms and legs ached with tiredness as he accepted his plate of beans and rice. Lolo carried his coffee, and Ignacio scooped up two extra tortillas for him. The soldier handing out the food didn't say a word as Nacio gestured with the tortillas at Uno's back.

They sat down to eat under their usual tree. It was nearly dark, but a few propane lanterns were scattered here and there so they could vaguely see each other. Once again they ate in silence, and even when the plates were empty they hadn't much to say.

Uno was still thinking about the afternoon. Here, shut up in a military camp, he had for the first time in his life felt completely whole, free, happy. Playing baseball, he had become a different person. He had not been hungry, tired, sick – not even lonely. I never felt this way before, he thought. It's a good feeling.

Behind them they heard a step, and when they looked around, they saw Mendoza. The captain was carrying a cup of coffee, and his face, though grave, was not forbidding.

The boys scrambled to their feet into what they hoped was "attention."

The captain nodded. "At ease." He glanced around at their three faces. "You men played well this afternoon. I can see we have some baseball talent here."

Nacio and Lolo smiled faintly. Uno dared to ask, "Sir – will we – be allowed to play again?"

Mendoza nodded. "On days when we can allow some recreation – yes. There aren't many of those, but you've all been working hard. And sometimes we all need to think of something besides the war."

At the word "war" all of their faces closed down. Uno felt as if the army had reached out and grabbed him all over again, and the pinpoint focus of drill and kill narrowed in front of him.

Then Mendoza turned to look directly at him. "You – Ramírez? – you're a pretty good player. Perhaps . . . some day . . . well, but first we have to win the war."

But as the captain turned to go, Uno suddenly blurted out, "Sir – one moment, please – I have thought of something –"

Mendoza turned, his face formal, as he once again became a commanding officer. "Yes?"

"Sir, if – no, *when* – we win the war – we should have baseball teams – every town should have a team – and we could have games – like in the U.S. –" And then he fell silent, stunned at his own audacity in suggesting – here in this place and now – that there might some day be a time when winning the war would not be the first effort, the only goal, of every man, woman, child.

Mendoza looked down at him. For the first time, and in spite of the captain's somber face, Uno looked back at him and felt that they were seeing – really seeing – each other. "Ah . . . yes," said the officer. He nodded only slightly, but still it was a nod. "Baseball. Baseball teams to play against each other. Instead of –"

"– instead of – shooting –"

Mendoza's eyes went deep and black. Uno knew at that moment he was not seeing Uno, or Nacio, or the other tired, dirty boys here on this lonely mountaintop, but other boys, other days. And other games, not war . . .

"Yes," said Mendoza. Then his shoulders straightened, and the deep black eyes became opaque again. "Some day. That is what we must do." And then he was gone.

Lolo and Nacio turned on him. "Where did you get that idea?"

Uno shook his head. "I don't know. I never thought of it until I said it –"

DAY FOUR

Once again the night passed with dreaming and waking. Uno found he was more used to the hard ground and the thin cover, which weren't much different from what he had always known, but now he was beginning to be conscious of the presence of the men around him more and more. Even though he could not see them at all during the dark hours, he felt them there. It was something like how he used to feel the village around him when he was still at home. Even if he couldn't see the other houses, the other people, he felt them there.

He wondered at this, and he wondered if the others felt it too. He decided to ask Lolo in the morning, because although he and Lolo often thought the same things, there were times when they didn't, and those times often explained a thing to him; it was like having two heads to think with instead of one.

But the fourth morning started like the others, and there was no time to talk. They pulled themselves out of their blankets, hurried through the latrines, and then there was a brief half-hour of drill with the rifles – loading, unloading, safeties on and off, and finally a short, hard drill on how to fall quickly and silently into a firing position.

Sergeant Díaz showed them how to raise the gun quickly and fire off a shot – and also to shift to automatic fire. Díaz called this latter operation "area fire." "If enough of you fire at one target, area fire will take it out." Or if there were time to prepare an attack or a defense, they learned how to flip down the little tripod attached to the rifle and fling themselves belly-down and legs spread on the ground so they had a more stable and less visible firing platform. Then he showed them the difference between a "high ready" position with the rifle as compared to one with the rifle held lower and the stock tucked into the armpit. They practiced moving forward both ways so they would know the difference in body balance. Even Uno found himself faintly, grudgingly impressed at how much there was to learn about this work of killing people.

When the drill was completed they were told to line up for food. Once again they received plates heaping with beans, tortillas, melon pieces, and cups of coffee. But as they sat down to eat in their usual spot, Juan came by with news.

"Don't waste any time here. Eat fast, roll your blankets. You'll be issued canteens and ammunition and some dry rations. We're to go on patrol with Captain Mendoza."

"Patrol?"

"We'll be gone a day or two – maybe three. Move!"

They shoveled their food in as quickly as they could, drank their coffee so fast it gurgled in their bellies. Then they scrambled back to where they had slept and grabbed up the blankets, shaking out dirt and twigs. While they were making a great dust and flap, Juan reappeared. He was loaded with supplies.

"Canteen for each of you," he grunted. "Fill them before we leave. Cup – spoon – bowl – dry rations –" He dumped these objects into their hands. "Roll the little stuff inside your blankets and then roll the hammocks all around it. Tie it with these ropes –"

Slapping and jabbing at them, Juan and Esteban – who came by to "help" – directed the rolling of the packs.

They filled their canteens at the truck that held the camp's water tank and then lined up at the Headquarters tent, prodded, as usual, by Juan. Ammunition – one clip for each gun – was handed out and the rifles loaded. By this time a party of ten men was assembled. Besides himself, Lolo, and Ignacio, Uno counted Juan, two experienced older men named García and Olivares, three men somewhat younger than García and Olivares but older than himself, who called each other Cedano, Estrada, and Ruiz, and Captain Mendoza.

They saluted sharply as the officer halted before them. He returned the salute.

"This morning," said Captain Mendoza, "we have received word that the loyalists are making moves toward the city of San Ildefonso. San Ildefonso has the television and radio stations, the best airfield, and the main railway depot, and all the main highways go through it. So far neither loyalists nor revolutionaries have gotten control of the city, although loyalists control most of the territory to the south of it. We've fought half a dozen times to gain control of the city, but we haven't been able to capture it. We can live – for a while – with San Ildefonso an open city, but not with it in loyalist hands." He paused and his eyes moved slowly from face to face. "I tell you these things so you will understand that we have to either keep the loyalists out of San Ildefonso or capture it ourselves. The revolution may well be decided by what happens here in this one city. Today I'm taking a patrol south toward the river to find out how many loyalist troops have come this far north and to see if we can find out what they plan to do next."

There was another moment of silence. One of the sergeants hurried up, saluted, handed Captain Mendoza a piece of paper. He read it, nodded, handed it back. The sergeant hurried away.

In the brief pause Uno stole a glance down at his rifle. Each man had loaded his weapon with the single clip, and Uno shifted the gun slightly to feel the change in weight and balance. That, even more than the captain's words, assured him that this was not just another drill. This was the real thing. He was so nervous he was shaking. He prayed he wouldn't wet his pants.

The captain turned back to them. "Each of you must understand why we are fighting this war. It is because we have no other choice left to us. I once read that an American president, John F. Kennedy, said, 'Those who make peaceful revolution impossible, make violent revolution inevitable.' If you don't understand this now, you will some day." He paused again and Uno thought that just for one instant he saw both weariness and grief through the formal mask the captain usually wore. "I deeply regret that some of you are still very new and your training has been brief. But war is like that. If life was such that each of us had what he needed, there would be no wars. Sergeant Díaz and I will lead you. We leave in ten minutes."

But it was with something like joy that Uno discovered they were to ride in a truck. Led again by Juan they hurried to a truck parked, motor rumbling, just inside the fortress gate. Uno scrambled up into the truck bed, clumsy with pack and rifle, but still with a secret thrill – a feeling of adventure and elation. If you had no choice but to be a soldier, at least it was a good thing to be a soldier in a truck. How many times, thought Uno, had he, Lolo, Ignacio, and all the others stood in the mud beside a cane field while trucks roared by and the armed men in them glared contemptuously down. Even though Uno had never expected nor wanted to be a soldier or fight in a war, still it would be nice to be one of those who rode and glared for a change.

It was the first time they had been out of the fortress since their arrival. Uno watched the gate swing open, then close behind them. For one moment he felt fiercely elated – "We're out!" – but that feeling quickly evaporated as he caught a cold glare from Sergeant Díaz. Uno quickly ironed out his face. Just like the packing shed, he thought.

Captain Mendoza rode in the cab of the truck, of course, and Uno could not hear anything he said, though the captain leaned out once or twice to peer across at an open space, and Uno saw his arms wave in gestures as he and the driver of the truck talked.

Uno wished he could stay closer to Mendoza, but he was

just a dumb recruit who was so useless he shouldn't even get in Mendoza's way. But Uno had a curious feeling about the captain that made him want to watch him, listen to him. Thinking of this made him recall his earlier remark about electing Mendoza president.

As the others stretched, scratched, talked among themselves, he said very quietly to Lolo, "It's funny – I never thought about electing presidents before we came here. Or baseball teams, or winning the war."

Lolo nodded. "Everything's different here. We're different."

"How?" Uno looked around him. "We just take orders, like we always did."

"Well . . . yes . . . but, no. It's different." Lolo paused and looked around guardedly, and Uno's eyes followed. Sergeant Díaz sat facing backward, and his eyes constantly searched the jungle, the road. Juan and Cedano were talking rifles, making gestures to illustrate features of other guns they knew about. Uno heard them describe a gun called an Uzi, another called AKM, and one, a Czech vz 58. Juan seemed to admire the Uzi; both agreed an Uzi would be good to have.

The other men talked quietly among themselves also. They seemed as ill assorted as a sackful of chickens, and yet, looking at them, Uno remembered how he had "felt" the presence of the men around him when he had waked up that morning, and he realized that now he "felt" them again. And, sitting there in the jolting, swaying truck, Uno suddenly knew that the feeling had to do with this – should any of them be attacked by anything – jungle-bred or human – the other nine would instantly counterattack in his support. And somewhere out on that damned hill or in that stinking jungle yesterday something had happened to him, because — he knew it now — *he* would attack too. He did not know why, or how it had happened, but he knew it.

"It's . . . it's . . ." Lolo was searching for words. They hadn't tried to figure out things like this before. "At home, we were just part of a family. A village. Here" — he waved vaguely — "we're part of . . . a country. *Our* country."

And that's different too, thought Uno. We never called it "our" country before.

And it was quite a while before he realized that they had stopped talking about escape.

After they had traveled half a dozen kilometers, Sergeant Díaz had four men post themselves as guards around the truck bed. They stood, braced against the jolting and swaying, two facing forward over the cab of the truck and one at each side halfway back. Their safeties were off, and their eyes never left the areas they were to watch, even when Cedano crawled to the back of the truck and vomited over the tailgate. Uno was glad that riding in the truck did not make him sick. He pictured in his mind how he would stand guard at the side or front if he were detailed and decided that war couldn't be all that bad if you rode into battle on a truck.

They jolted perhaps five more kilometers down the slope of the mountain on the narrow, rain-rutted track through scattered patches of trees. As they descended, the air began to feel warmer and the scents of the jungle began to reach them. Soon they were on a flatter road and the jungle quickly closed in as if to choke off the narrow track. Then, suddenly, they felt the brakes grab, and the truck skidded to a halt in what seemed a very small clearing. The trees met overhead, and the understory was a thick green wall.

"Out!"

As those ahead of him scrambled toward the back and over the tailgate Uno shot a questioning glance at Lolo. Lolo shrugged. Maybe they weren't going to ride into battle after all, Uno thought. There was certainly no sign of another human being, friend or enemy, here.

After unloading their equipment they assembled beside the road. Then they heard the truck driver shift gears. He wheeled left, reversed, shifted into low gear, and a second later, with a roar, the truck was plowing back up the road toward the fortress, away from them.

Uno watched it go with a sinking feeling. He had liked being in the truck. He did not like being on the ground again. Important men rode in trucks. Dumb damn peasants walked. He hoped he would get to ride in a truck again, no matter where it went.

Díaz waited till the noise of the truck died away so he would not have to shout. As it disappeared through the jungle, he stepped forward and flipped a blanket off a couple of piles of equipment. "Sling your packs on your backs and carry rifles at the ready. You – Ruiz – carry the extra ammunition. García, the rocket launcher."

Uno was momentarily distracted by the sight of the rocket

launcher. It had a mean, capable look, like a very small dog who was known to be a vicious fighter. García, who hoisted it onto his shoulder, was an older man, experienced, plainly one who knew his way around in a war. Uno thought it might be worthwhile to stay near and watch him, but Juan cut him off when he tried to fall in line behind García. Juan's eyes never left García – or rather the rocket launcher.

Sergeant Díaz led them out of the clearing, and they immediately plunged into trackless jungle. Even following in a tight line it was hard to keep track of the man ahead and the one behind. Leaves slapped their faces, vines snagged their feet, flies and mosquitoes rose in blinding clouds that swarmed around their faces. Uno forgot the joy of the truck as his feet slid over the rotting vegetation and slippery mud of the jungle floor. Damn, he said to himself, as he drifted farther and farther back in the line, it was a short ride and a long walk.

For two hours they slogged on through the jungle. Even though Díaz called short breaks at intervals for them to rest, the journey seemed endless. Although Uno had lived on the fringe of the jungle all his life, he had never spent so much time actually in it as he had these last two or three days. He knew the trees, the birds, the greasy moisture. But most of his time before had been spent either cutting cane, working in the fields, or loading bananas on the fruit ships. On the docks at least the sea wind came down the coastline to flutter the leaves of the palm trees and ripple the water and cool your face.

Around noon Díaz called a halt. Uno, stumbling along at the end of the line, was the last one to crash through the vines and fall to the ground beside the others. Díaz, he saw with rage, did not even appear to be tired.

"Drink some water," Díaz directed them. "And eat a little. Save some rations for tonight and tomorrow. We won't get any more, except for water, until we get back to the fortress."

Uno opened his pack, unscrewed the cap on the canteen, and took a drink. The water was warm and had a rusty taste, but it was better than no water at all. In any case, the well water they drank at the village often stank of excrement, so rust did not taste all that bad. He opened some small packs of very dry bread and a can of beans and ate. Lolo and Ignacio, on either side of him, crammed food in as he did, like hungry animals.

No one spoke while they ate – it seemed to be commonly agreed that food here was so rare and precious as to require one's full attention. And indeed, Uno knew enough about the jungle to know that if you wanted to starve, a jungle was the best place to do it. The village gardens and farms produced very little food from their poor, thin soil and the jungle almost none. Apart from a little meat that occupied the canopy seventy feet above their heads – birds and monkeys – and the occasional fruit tree, the jungle was the most foodless place you could find. Made you wonder, thought Uno, why anyone would fight a war to control such a land. What we should all do is leave it to the monkeys and get on a boat and go and live in some other country –

Sergeant Díaz and Captain Mendoza had sat down together

so they could eat and examine some maps at the same time. They talked briefly but not loud enough for anyone else to hear. Uno wished he could find out what was going to happen, but he doubted if he could learn any more even if he did manage to catch a word or two.

García, the man who had carried the rocket launcher, sat braced against the trunk of a tree, with Juan and two others quite near. Juan stared hungrily at the rocket launcher. Uno remembered that Juan had boasted he would be sent to a school somewhere to learn about artillery. Looking now at his fellow soldiers with their mismatched uniforms and rifles, and the sole item that could be called a serious weapon – the rocket launcher – Uno wondered if this army really had any artillery or a place to train soldiers to use it. So far as he could see, "training" in this army of the revolution consisted of being kidnapped from your home and thrown into the company of dangerous men, most of whom were probably thieves and murderers, or would be if they weren't in the army. Then you were handed a stolen gun with a couple of days' instructions on how not to shoot yourself or the man next to you, most of whom were as half-ass stupid as you were. Considering what he had seen this far, Uno began to suspect that Juan was as close to "artillery school" right now as he was ever going to get.

Suddenly a sound cut through the thick walls of the jungle. It was a ragged tearing sound – *machine-gun fire.*

Díaz and Mendoza hissed for silence, but the men were already frozen. Díaz dropped a hand, and all of them slid off whatever they were sitting on and melted into cover at ground level. As he sank into a pool of fern fronds, Uno was astonished to see, looking around, that even at this close range he could not see men whom he knew weren't more than ten meters away.

In the silence the staccato chatter of the weapons came again. Díaz, to his left, indicated, "East."

Mendoza nodded. The firing went on, broke off, began again. Uno tried to figure out how far away it was, but he didn't know enough about weapons or their sound to calculate. It must have been some distance — two or three hundred meters — though, because neither Díaz nor Mendoza had signaled them to retreat.

There was another pause in the firing. Díaz inched over to Mendoza, and they whispered together. In another moment Mendoza rose to a crouching position and began to move off in the direction of the shooting. He moved fast. Díaz silently ticked off one man after another, and soon the whole squad was moving like shadows through the jungle, with Díaz bringing up the rear.

Uno was behind García and ahead of Lolo. Juan was just behind Lolo, and Uno knew if he made so much as a leaf fall or a twig snap, Juan would be on him like a boa constrictor. Sweating and tense he slid between vines and over roots like a fer-de-lance stalking prey. He kept his rifle out of the mud but pointed away from García as he tried to remember what they were supposed to have learned about firing positions. Trying to hold the high ready position made his arms ache; then, just as he felt that his trembling arms would let the gun drop, the line ahead came to a halt.

For a moment he could see nothing. Then, as he lowered

himself to a kneeling position, he found a hole in the leaves through which he could see ahead.

They were on the edge of a clearing. The squad was still hidden in the trees, but directly ahead lay an open space of several square hectares, with a cluster of little mud and thatch houses, some scratchy gardens, pigs, a few chickens searching listlessly through the litter.

Uno's eyes swept the place. It was the kind of village he had lived in all his life. Even though he had never seen it before he knew exactly where the well would be located and how the trails would lead to the next village.

But the people who should have been there working in the gardens, tending the pigs and chickens – where were they? There was now a heavy stillness about the place. The guns had ceased firing; there were no voices, not even a bird call or a dog barking.

Uno's heart began to thud in his chest. He felt fresh sweat begin to pour down his back and the insides of his thighs. Why was the silence now so much more ominous than the sound of gunfire had been?

There was a quiver in the leaves ahead of him, and Uno realized they were on the move again. Once again it was the silent glide from tree to tree, breathless, barely daring to wipe off sweat from his face. Carefully, carefully, now they moved in a mottled green line circling around the clearing, always just inside the screen of the jungle.

Slowly the rest of the village was revealed as they worked their way around it.

And now on the far side they found the people.

And they learned why the village was silent.

Sprawled on the ground were the bodies of three – eight – eleven people. Bright red fountains of blood rose out of them as if pumped out, and here and there a hand twitched, a foot jerked. Once a child – a little boy – cried out, but immediately fell silent with a bubbling sigh.

In the center of the bodies was a stick thrust into the ground, and on it was a banner made of striped cloth. Orange and white bars fluttered above the red blood.

Behind him Juan grunted. "Flag," he said. "That's how they mark their kills. That's a loyalist flag."

Uno crouched frozen where he had dropped. His heart was pounding, and he wanted to scream – but of course men did not do that. He made no sound, although his breath seemed to whistle, going in and out of his chest.

All around him the men were so silent they could hear flies buzzing as they appeared out of nowhere to circle around the bodies, drawn by the smell of blood. There was no wind, and the only thing moving was a vulture, already scenting death, turning in slow circles high above them.

Then Captain Mendoza slapped Díaz very lightly on the back. Díaz rose to a crouch and ran around the edge of the clearing to where a foot trail entered the jungle. Running lightly he disappeared around the first curve. Moments passed and there was no command for the rest of them to move. One of the wounded – a woman – groaned a little, and Uno, hearing her, made an involuntary movement to rise and go to her. García, on his right, swung a hand out to stop him.

Uno sank back into position, but his mind was exploding.

"García," he whispered, "they're dying. Why don't we help them? Maybe we could save – there's a little boy –"

"Captain –" They jerked around. It was Díaz back from his brief reconnaisance. "Loyalist patrol – seven men. Maybe half a kilometer ahead on the trail –"

Mendoza stood up, motioned the men quickly forward. As his eyes raked over them Uno knew he would pick his best men to attack the patrol. "Olivares! See to the victims. Díaz – take García," he said crisply. "Leave the rocket launcher here – and take Juan, Estrada, Cedano, Ruiz. Move fast. I don't want one of those bastards to live. And search them for maps –"

García laid the rocket launcher down, and by the time he had it covered with a plastic sheet the others had gone so far he had to run to catch up. In seconds all six vanished into the jungle.

Mendoza watched them go. "Good hunting," he said softly. Then he turned to the others. "Come."

Olivares was already moving from one bloody form to another. "They are all dead, Captain," he said quietly.

Mendoza motioned them to advance. Uno rose to his feet, and as they neared the eleven bodies he felt his breath stop and his legs turn to water. He had never imagined anything so terrible as this. He had seen dead people before – people in the village who had died of disease or accident – but he had been allowed to see them only when they were washed and ready for the coffin. Even the men who bled to death from machete wounds, even the children who died of diarrhea, the women who died in childbirth – none of them looked like this.

The first two bodies were old women. Their skulls had been crushed. Four men – all old men with scrawny, bent bodies that looked like brown, carved wood – lay in a half circle facing the jungle. They had sticks nearby as if they had tried to defend their village with cattle prods. Behind them, nearer the huts, lay two women, younger, and, near them, the little boy and two girls who looked like sisters.

In the middle of the battleground Uno stopped. He clenched his hands and wept. He could not help it. He could not stop. He knew that Mendoza and Díaz and the others would surely punish him, but he could not stop.

Lolo gave him a sharp push. "Quiet," he said. "Shut up. Or Captain Mendoza will –"

"Leave him alone." It was Olivares speaking. Olivares was the only experienced soldier whom Mendoza had kept with him now, with the recruits, Uno, Lolo, and Ignacio.

Uno and Lolo turned bleak faces to Olivares.

The older man said quietly, "Captain Mendoza says that if a man feels grief, then he must grieve. I have seen this too many times. I grieve inside myself. But someone *must* grieve – someone *must* weep – for them."

Suddenly Uno found his voice. "What good does grieving do?" he screamed.

Mendoza appeared from one of the little huts. He was carrying a spade and a length of grass matting. "It is grief," he said quietly, "that makes us fight this revolution."

They dug the graves with sweat pouring down their faces. Captain Mendoza directed them to locate the graves in a corn field near the huts where the earth was already soft. No one, he said, would grow corn here for a long time to come.

The captain sent Uno to remove sticks from the fence that bordered the clearing and showed him how to trim and bind them with bits of rope into crosses. As Uno struggled to make eleven crosses that would hold up straight and not fold into limp X shapes, there were bitter questions crashing around in his mind: Why did the loyalists kill them? Why didn't they just steal the pigs and chickens and any money they had — and let them live? Why did they kill the children? Why — why — *why* did they kill the little boy?

The boy — Uno had taken one swift, sick look — had been about the same age as his baby brothers. And the memory of his family rose up like a red tide in him. My mother — Concepción — the babies — are they all right? Or are they — ?

Lolo appeared at his elbow. His face was very still, and his hands hardly shook as he picked up the first cross. "When they are all buried, Captain Mendoza says we will pray."

"What for?" bawled Uno. "They're dead!"

Lolo nodded. "Hurry with the crosses."

"I can't," choked Uno. "They won't hold straight —"

Then as Lolo went away with the first cross, Captain Mendoza appeared beside Uno. He was carrying a machete, and he leaned down, picked up the fence sticks Uno had collected, and began to make notches in them. Uno watched silently as Mendoza prepared the sticks in pairs — one short, one long — and tossed them at his feet. Silently Uno assembled the crosses, a long upright and a short crossarm, and began to bind them together.

"If we had got here sooner —" Uno said suddenly.

Mendoza nodded wearily. "Yes. Of course."

"Why didn't we –"

"We didn't know the patrol was this far north. This is what we came to find out. But we expected to intercept them tomorrow – farther south. It was too late the moment we heard the first shots."

Uno stared down at the crosses, all of which were now ready. "This – isn't – *enough!*" he whispered. "What is a cross? Just two sticks of wood! They need – they need something more –"

Captain Mendoza glanced at him quietly. "Díaz," he said, "has gone to . . . punish the loyalists."

Uno, squatting there beside the pile of crosses, said, "Yes – Díaz is a good soldier. He can fight. He can at least make them pay for what they did. But the people – they needed help – they needed soldiers here *before* – to drive the loyalists off –" He halted, staring up at the captain's bleak face as if to demand an answer, a reason why quite ordinary people had been slaughtered. "We got here too late. Now all we can do" – he made a futile gesture at his pile of sticks – "now all we can do is make crosses for babies – for old grandmothers – who were murdered. What good are *crosses?*"

Captain Mendoza turned to look at the little village, which both of them knew would now go back to jungle. "What good are crosses?" he sighed. "All I know is that in this war there will be many crosses. Each one of us will have his own. I carry mine. You will carry yours. And it takes crosses to make the revolution. And a new nation – in which people like these" – he nodded at the bodies – "will have a better life. That's all I can tell you about crosses."

*

Mendoza had Olivares and the boys take turns with the grave-digging. The graves had to be deep – "because of the pigs," Mendoza told them – but only wide enough for the bodies. There were no coffins and no time or tools with which to build any.

"They ought to have coffins," grunted Uno as his turn came to dig. He thrust the spade into the soil between rows of cornstalks. At this season, the corn had been harvested and only a few broken stalks were left. "Even at home when someone died we always had a coffin," he muttered. "And flowers to lay on it. And we all marched in procession to the graveyard. And sometimes a priest was there. Or old Señor Calderon said the prayers. We never just buried people in the ground like this –"

Lolo, who had dug one grave, was resting in the shade of a hut. "I thought we were poor then. Maybe it's just because I am gone and I remember it – but now our village looks rich to me," he said as he stared around at the silent village.

"Rich?" Ignacio said from inside one of the huts where he was helping Captain Mendoza locate mats or rags to wrap the corpses in. "You think we were rich? You're crazy. We were hungry – sick – none of you went to school more than two years. You call that rich?"

"He means – *alive*. Not rich." Uno thrust up a spadeful of the thin, poor soil and tossed it on a growing pile. "That's the difference between our village and this one. Our people are alive."

"At least we . . . think they are." Lolo stared wearily at the corn field. "We don't even know that."

Suddenly Uno felt a wave of cold despair wash over him. "They have to be. They have to be." But he knew that his own village could be laid waste just as easily as this one. The war could sweep over it too, and there would be no one there to defend it. All at once he was gripped by an idea. "I have a gun now – I could go back. If they are attacked –"

"The gun belongs to the army of the revolution," said Ignacio. "And if you run off with so much as a match or an empty cartridge they'll shoot you in the back. No – you aren't going back to defend our village."

"Then – who – *will?*"

Ignacio shrugged. "I don't know. I hope . . . we have to hope . . . that what they tell us is true. That this army" – he glanced around at the few soldiers he could see – "that this army will do what it says it will do. Feed people. Make a better country."

"*This* army?" muttered Uno, just loud enough for Ignacio to hear. "You mean soldiers like Juan, Esteban, Whistler? This army is a bunch of –"

"I know that."

"And we can trust them to take care of our families?"

"We have to. Who else . . . is there?"

They stared bleakly at each other. It's true, Uno thought. Bad as this army is – it's probably the best this country's ever seen. "Shit," he muttered.

"Yeah," said Ignacio.

There was some thumping and scraping inside one of the huts, and in a moment Captain Mendoza emerged. Ignacio came out too, carrying a few grass mats and some other things. He distributed the mats among the bodies. "There aren't enough mats, Captain Mendoza," he said. "But there are some scraps of cloth here."

"Do the best you can," said Mendoza. "Wrap them and we will lay them in the graves. When Díaz gets back we will close the graves and pray over them."

Ignacio and Olivares took the mats and began to arrange the bodies on them, wrapping and tying them with vines cut just inside the jungle's edge.

"Prayers," grunted Ignacio as he worked, "won't do much good here. What they needed was guns. Some oxen to plow with. A good well for clean water. And food to eat. This man" – he gestured at the corpse of the old man they were laying out on a mat – "he never had enough to eat. His teeth are gone. His ribs stick out. He had a crooked leg because he broke it and it wasn't set right. What good does prayer do? Did prayer to God save these people?"

Olivares straightened the old man's ragged cotton pants and shirt. "God didn't kill these people," he said. "Don't blame him."

"Well, somebody is to blame." Ignacio finished his last knot, and together they lifted the old man's body and carried it across the blood-soaked ground to lower it carefully into one of the graves. "*We* must be to blame. We should have gotten here sooner. We should have shot those loyalist butchers before they could do this."

"We kill all the loyalists we can find," said Olivares mildly. "How many bullets have you fired? And when did you join us in this struggle? Only when we came to your village and . . . recruited you."

Ignacio stared around him. "I had heard of things like this.

I had never seen it myself. But my parents were *desaparecidos*. I was trying to work out some way to stay alive – maybe get to the capital and look for them. I read everything I could – newspapers –"

"Read?" Captain Mendoza looked up suddenly from another body. "You can read?"

"I read well, Captain," said Ignacio with a faint smile. "My mother was a schoolteacher, my father was a doctor before the loyalists arrested them. My mother taught me some English, and my father made me learn the names of the bones, the arteries, other things. And I've been to school more than these other two." He nodded toward Uno and Lolo. "I wanted to be a doctor too. But, of course, there is no hope of that now."

There was a brief silence, unnoticed by anyone but Uno, who happened at that moment to be looking at Captain Mendoza. Uno saw a flicker of expression cross the officer's face, and suddenly he felt that the captain had made a decision about something – maybe about Ignacio. But the captain only said, "Díaz should be back soon. When we have finished here" – they all looked around at the haunted village – "we must move on."

They had all eleven bodies wrapped and lying in the open graves and the crosses placed ready to mount at each grave and still Díaz had not returned.

Ignacio worried about Díaz. "I wonder why he's not back? They didn't have that far to go to catch up, he said. And I haven't heard any gunshots."

"You couldn't hear that far," said Olivares. "And anyway . . . he might not shoot them."

Ignacio jerked a look at Olivares, started to say something, and then was silent. Olivares nodded slightly, then leaned his head back to rest against the wall of the hut where both of them had taken shelter from the hot sun.

Uno was listening, but he was less concerned about Díaz than about the bodies they had just prepared for burial. "Pigs will dig them up," he worried, "if they aren't buried deep. We should find logs or stones to cover them. The little boy . . ." He broke off. Every time he had looked at the child he had seen the face of one of his brothers.

"He is with God," said Olivares.

No. He's with me, thought Uno. He'll be with me always.

Lolo was rubbing at some smears of blood on his hands. He glanced sideways at the captain and finally said, "Sir. Do the loyalists always do this?" He nodded at the village.

Captain Mendoza rubbed his forehead. "Not always. But this territory has been supporting us. Sometimes the loyalists wipe out a village just to warn the others."

"So if *we* weren't here –" Lolo spoke too suddenly, then choked himself off.

"Yes. If there were no revolutionary army this wouldn't have happened. Instead of being shot, they could have just gone on dying of pneumonia and measles and diarrhea and bad water and starvation. Is that what you want for them? For yourselves?"

"No –"

"Well, those are the choices. Either starve slowly – and

watch your children die — or die quickly in a war. We know what happens without the war. But we know — we believe — that we can make things better — when we *win* the war —"

At the end of an hour, when Díaz and his men had not yet returned, Captain Mendoza ordered them to close the graves. They had found only one spade and had to take turns with it, although Lolo and Ignacio found pieces of wood with which they helped to scrape the loose dirt over the bodies.

Uno stood at the edge of the burial ground, trying to swallow his nausea and help the others. But every time he advanced toward one of the graves he felt the acid rise in his mouth and he had to back off.

Captain Mendoza was busy setting a cross at each grave, but he saw Uno's struggle and said, "Go into the jungle — not too far — and see if you can find some ferns — even some leaves. Lay them on the graves after they are closed. Leave your rifle here."

Uno leaned his rifle against the wall of a hut where Lolo's and Ignacio's rifles were stacked — Olivares had now been detailed to stand watch over the burial party — and turned to go. As he passed Lolo they glanced at each other. He had expected that Lolo would signal contempt at his weakness, but Lolo's face was curiously blank. Lolo nodded. "Be careful," he said quietly.

Uno nodded bleakly. He crossed the clearing, and as the margin of trees closed around him he hoped for once that he would put his foot down on a fer-de-lance. At least then he would die quickly and never have to spend another day wondering when he would see another village like this one or if his own village was now a stinking, rotting pool of blood and bodies.

As he moved along inside the verge of the jungle it was suffocatingly hot, but very quiet. Since it was nearly the end of the dry season there were no flowers, but he gathered some small branches of shrubs with pretty leaves. At last he broke off several fern fronds. Altogether he had a huge armful as he turned back to the village.

His search had taken him on a course roughly parallel to the edge of the village fields, and he was now almost directly opposite the point at which they had entered the village just after the shooting. He paused for a moment, staring out of the gloom of the forest and into the burning bright basin of sunlight in the clearing. "This whole country is a jungle," he said to himself, "with just a few villages. Someday all the villages will be gone and only the jungle will be left for jaguars and wild pigs –"

Across the small fields he could see Lolo and the others finishing the burials. They were working on the last one, the little boy's grave, and suddenly he couldn't look anymore. He turned away, facing back into the jungle –

– and saw her.

A girl. Ten, maybe twelve years old. She was wounded – there was blood down the front of her blue cotton dress – and she lay crumpled at the foot of a tree, staring at him with eyes like night. All this he saw in a fraction of an instant.

For a moment they froze – neither spoke.

Then Uno dropped the ferns and leaped across to the girl. "God!" he cried. "How did you – who are you? From the village? Are you – you're hurt!"

She stared up at him, rigid with fear.

Uno dropped to his knees beside her. He reached out but instantly realized that he could not carry her back to the village. She was as big as he was. Then he jumped up, ran to the edge of the trees. "Captain! Captain Mendoza!" he shouted. "I have found someone – here – alive!"

He ran back to the girl but stopped short. She looked as if she wanted to try to get away, but if she struggled, he could see that her wound, already bleeding heavily, might hemorrhage even worse. The blood was even soaking down into a bundle of rags which she held clenched to her breast.

"Don't – don't be afraid," he told her hurriedly. "We will take care of you. The captain – he is a good man –"

At that moment he heard the sound of footsteps, and in another second the captain burst through the screen of the jungle. Lolo and the others were at his heels.

"A girl!" cried Lolo. "How did she get here?"

Captain Mendoza knelt quickly beside the girl. "Don't be afraid – we won't hurt you. I'm Captain Mendoza – we are revolutionaries – I am so sorry we got here too late –"

The girl stared up at all of them, dazed, almost fainting. Then slowly, as if her strength was almost gone with the blood seeping from her body, she whispered, "I am Magdalena Sánchez. My family lives here. Where . . . is my father?"

Captain Mendoza hesitated. Then he said, "Magdalena, we must put you on a stretcher and take you back to one of the huts. We can take care of your wound there and decide what to do with you. You can't stay here."

Olivares had already set to work snapping off some bamboo poles with his machete. Then he had Ignacio and Lolo take off their shirts and ran the poles through the sleeves. He laid the rough litter on the ground. "Ready, Captain."

Together Olivares and Mendoza lifted the girl to the stretcher and picked it up. "Well, Ramírez," grunted the captain, "it's a good thing I sent you for ferns. Otherwise this child would have died here. Sometimes it pays to be a bad soldier —"

They carried the girl around to the side of the village away from the graves and into one of the huts. Uno followed, after gathering up his load of ferns. As Olivares and Mendoza laid the stretcher down the girl winced and Uno, standing at the open door, saw fresh blood ooze down her breast. But in spite of her obvious pain, she clenched the very small bundle of rags close to her as she glared at them.

"I didn't let them get him —" she whispered.

Captain Mendoza had knelt beside her to examine her wound. His eyes jerked back to her face. "Him?" he asked quickly.

"I didn't let them get him —" the girl said again, urgently, feverish in the way her hands like wild things clutched the rags.

Captain Mendoza reached out and grabbed the edge of the rag and flipped it back. A fuzzy round black ball about the size of a boy's fist came into view and beneath that a tiny face –

"Baby!" said Captain Mendoza sharply. "My God – it's a baby!"

They stared at the child. "Captain –" whispered Olivares – "is it – alive?"

The captain reached out, slid a finger beneath the rags, but at that moment the tiny face wrinkled into a grimace and a faint squeak came out. "It's alive," said the captain. "Child" – he laid his hand briefly on the girl's cheek – "whose baby is it? Where did you find –"

"My brother. He was born only this morning," the girl said, though she seemed to be oblivious to anything said to her. "I helped her – my mother. I am a woman myself – I know about these things. I did a good job – my mother said so –" Then the girl began to struggle, as if to rise. She put a hand out as if to emphasize to the captain that she had indeed done a good job. "It was my mother's seventh baby – we have lost four babies – and I wanted to help her and make sure this baby lived –"

"Yes, yes," said Mendoza quickly. "Yes, he is a fine baby. We can see that. But now lie down – you're bleeding." He and Ignacio tried to coax the girl to lay back down on the stretcher. Olivares had disappeared for a moment but now returned with a few bandages and some antiseptic in a bottle.

"Captain," said Olivares, "we've got to see if there is a bullet in her, get a compress on the wound –"

"Ramírez," said Captain Mendoza, "come here. Hold the baby –"

But the girl screamed when they took the child from her arms. Uno knew she had not screamed like that – nor screamed at all – when she was shot. To calm her, he took the tiny baby in his arms and sat down very close to the girl. He held the baby, who squirmed and squeaked a little, close to the girl's face so she could see him. "Be quiet," he said. "Let them bandage your wound. The baby is here. He is all right. See?"

Her breath came in ragged gasps as she stared at the baby's face. She seemed not to notice at all as Olivares laid back her torn dress, examined the wound, and swabbed it with antiseptic.

"No bullet that I can see," said Olivares. "Looks like it went through the muscle at the top of her shoulder. I can't tell – may have nicked the bone too." He poured antiseptic on the area where the bullet had entered and where it had left her body. Then he covered the wounds with pads of gauze and bound the dressing on with strips of cloth Ignacio had found in a corner beside some cooking pots.

"We are going to call him Manolete," the girl said weakly. "My mother said Manolete was a brave bullfighter once in Spain, so she wanted the baby to have a brave name. I can't wait to show him to my father – and my little brother. Where are they? And where is my mother –"

Mendoza and Olivares, finishing the last knot on the dressing, glanced up. As their eyes met, Captain Mendoza said, "We can't do that right now, Magdalena. Perhaps – later –"

The girl seemed to drift off then, as if she had fallen into a light doze, rousing every few minutes to murmur a few words.

"My mother . . . so happy . . . a boy . . ."

For a moment Captain Mendoza and Olivares watched the bandages to see if the bleeding would continue. Then Olivares smoothed the girl's dress over the bandages and they both stood up.

"That's the best we can do for her now," said the captain. "We'll leave her here to rest. Ramírez – you stay here with her. If she wakes up she may cry out, try to get up. Watch her."

The captain, followed by the others, turned and left the hut.

Uno watched them go. "Yes, sir," he muttered automatically. Then, as he saw Lolo and Nacio turn to the left to resume work on the graves, he acknowledged bleakly that it was probably a good thing Captain Mendoza had ordered him to stay with the girl. "Go to sleep, Manolete," he said to the baby. "Captain Mendoza sent the good soldiers out to check on the war. I've been left here to take care of you. That's all I'm good for. Go to sleep."

But the baby, strangely awake and strangely calm, lay quietly among his rags, eyes wide open and watching Uno as if Uno were the most important thing he would ever see. His tiny face was grave and thoughtful.

Uno stared down at him. "I don't blame you," he said. "You are probably right to stay awake. I would advise you to do that too. They only left me with you because I am the worst soldier they have. You are right to keep an eye on me –"

Díaz returned an hour later with the five men in his detail. They were all curiously silent, even Juan, and Mendoza did not question them much. They brought no prisoners, but they had a dozen rifles, some ammunition, canteens of water, a few packages of dry rations, and one map. It was hand-drawn and appeared to have fictitious names for real places, but both Mendoza and Díaz seemed to recognize the territory it covered.

Captain Mendoza, Olivares, and Díaz settled on their haunches beside the open door of the hut where Uno still sat with the girl and the baby. As they huddled over the map, Mendoza, with a sharp look at Díaz, said, "Did you learn anything else?"

Díaz laid his rifle across his knees and looked up with a face as bland as butter. "Just a patrol, Captain, like us. We did not find out where the main force is, but we think they are to the west. On the other side of the river."

"Why? Why to the west?"

"Because the loyalists acted like they would escape in that direction. If they could."

Uno, sitting silently beside the sleeping girl, listened to this report and pictured the scene in his mind. Escape to the west, he thought. I suppose that means the loyalists were running in that direction when Díaz –

"Ran them down and gutted the bastards," Lolo said suddenly behind him. Uno turned in time to see Lolo slide through the open window and drop beside him and the girl. "They killed every one of them. After they . . . questioned them."

"You mean, tortured them."

"Uno," Lolo said irritably, "what do you think the loyalists would do to *us* if they captured this patrol? What did the loyalists do to these people" – he waved a hand to indicate the death-struck village – "and they weren't even soldiers!"

Uno stared down at the baby's face. The child had finally finished his sober evaluation of his new-found world and gone to sleep. The girl slept too, twitching and moaning from time to time. "I know," said Uno. "I know. Lolo . . . what would we do . . . if we got captured. And . . . tortured?"

There was a heavy silence. They stared at each other over the baby's fuzzy head.

At last Lolo spoke. "I . . . don't know. It could happen. I would try to stand it."

"What if you" – and suddenly Uno thought about the rooster, Saint Peter's rooster, and he realized there was a lot more to that rooster than he had thought – "what if you . . . couldn't? And you . . . talked. Gave – information. What if people got killed, because you" – he was talking about himself, of course – "because you talked?"

Lolo straightened up, and his face closed down as if he had decided to shut a door on something he did not want to look at. "It could happen. You'd be all right. Don't think about it." He turned and slid back through the window.

Don't think about it? Uno thought, staring after him. How can I help thinking about it? For just one moment pictures – words – he had heard about people being tortured flashed through his mind.

But then – even worse – was the idea that he might not be strong enough to stand it.

The rooster – he told himself – I don't want that rooster to crow for me . . .

*

In the late afternoon, with the sun sinking nearly to the tops of the trees, Mendoza called them to attention. They stood in a fairly straight line – Uno also – and listened silently as the captain recited a short prayer service beside the graves. The ferns and leaves Uno had brought from the jungle lay across the narrow mounds like splashes of green paint. The leaves were already wilted, and by tomorrow the jungle heat would have shriveled them to colorless fragments. The graves, though raw and new now, would quickly sink down and be overgrown by weeds and vines, and the village itself would disappear in a season or two as the jungle reclaimed the land.

Uno listened to the prayers and made the sign of the cross, but he was not praying inside himself. This isn't enough. They deserve more than this, he kept repeating in his mind.

After the service was finished Mendoza began preparing the patrol to leave. The two survivors of the raid, he said, would have to be carried with them, though he did not indicate what his plans, if any, might be for their care. The makeshift stretcher had been strengthened with some ropes, and the girl, moving restlessly and somewhat delirious, was tied on it so she would not throw herself off. Guns and other equipment were parceled out so each man carried a share. Olivares wrapped the baby in a scrap of cloth and, with a feeding bottle made of a tin of canned milk and a rag wick, settled him on his left arm. In his right arm he carried his own rifle and two of the captured rifles.

Juan, who had been silent since his return with Díaz, glanced at Uno and Lolo as the extra arms were divided. "So, little soldiers, what have *you* accomplished while we were gone?"

Uno and Lolo stared flatly back at him. Uno was greatly relieved when Lolo came up with the only answer: "We followed the captain's orders." Juan turned away.

Mendoza looked them over as they readied themselves for the return march. "We failed to save the village," he said quietly, with deep regret. "I only wish we could have gotten here in time. But we did get some of the information we had to have. Now we must return to the fortress. It will be a hard march — we'll have to make several kilometers before dark."

As the ragged line of men filed across the clearing and into the jungle, Uno turned for a last look. For one awful moment his heart felt as if it would burst out of his chest with grief. I won't forget — he told the sleeping village — I will never — never — forget you —

It appeared from the direction they now took that Mendoza was leading them back to the fortress by a different, more circuitous route. As the sun dropped lower the line of men moved quietly through the jungle, advancing northwestward, but now, burdened by the wounded girl and the infant and the extra equipment, they made poor time. The girl was quiet for the most part, but the baby cried weakly from time to time.

All of the older men took turns carrying the stretcher. Uno and Lolo were not asked to carry the stretcher, but they were loaded till their knees buckled with the extra rifles and ammunition. Uno had thought the effort coming down from the fortress had been difficult; he now looked upon it as child's play as he watched his feet sink into the mud to the ankles under the weight he carried.

When Mendoza called a halt he sank to the ground where his last step took him. In the gathering darkness camp was made quickly. García hacked a circle out of the undergrowth with his machete and Olivares took care to search the area for snakes, ants, and spiny plants. All of the men found places where they could string up their hammocks. Mendoza instructed Ignacio to cut a small amount of dry wood – if he could find some close by – and build a fire. Uno and Lolo were told to stack the rifles in the center of the clearing beside the ammunition and other supplies and to get some ferns to cushion the girl's stretcher. Uno found himself holding the baby, who for some reason seemed to cry less in his care.

When the camp was safely in order, Captain Mendoza directed Uno to get the can of milk from Olivares's pack and sit down to feed the child. Juan glanced over at him as he helped secure a plastic sheet over the ammunition. "Nursey-nursey," he said softly. "He thinks you're his mother."

Uno glared at him. "He just knows I'm smart enough not to drop him on his head."

Mendoza called García and Olivares, and they gathered beside the fire to consult some of the maps they had brought with them. Juan was careful to squat far enough away so as not to give the appearance of being where he had not been ordered to be but close enough to establish the fact that he was one of the regular soldiers and not one of the baby-sitters.

Uno noted this and promised himself that he would find a way to "out-soldier" Juan in something, if it took him the whole war to do it.

Ignacio's fire, though small, made a faint red glow that highlighted the men's faces and glinted off the rifle barrels. Mendoza was making plans for the next day and outlining their duties to García and Olivares. Their voices were so low, however, that even from a few feet away Uno could hear nothing. He wondered if Mendoza intended to go into a fire fight carrying a girl and a baby. Finally the officer made some notes and calculations on the margins of the maps and studied them. He nodded two or three times, and it appeared that he was satisfied with the amount of information the patrol had so far gathered.

When the map study was finished Olivares took a few packages of the dry rations and boiled some rice and coffee in a couple of tin pots. Each man hastily produced his cup, spoon, and bowl, and Olivares parceled out the food. Lolo helped Uno arrange his food on the ground in front of him and even offered to blow on his coffee to cool it.

Then Olivares prepared a bowl for the girl and gave it to Mendoza. The captain carried the rice to the girl where she lay at the edge of the circle and knelt beside her. She was half conscious now, and the captain raised the spoon to her lips. She ate reluctantly, but he got most of the bowlful down her. Then Olivares refilled the bowl and the captain ate.

When the rice had been eaten, they broke open some packets of the dry bread and ate it with the coffee. Uno felt he had never appreciated food so much in his whole life as he had since the revolutionaries conscripted him. He separated the grains of rice in his mouth just to feel them, fat and tender, and tasted every crumb of the bread. He let the coffee slosh around in his mouth so he could experience every bit of its flavor, the sharp brown bite of it. "Good," he sighed, "good."

Most of the time they kept talk to a minimum and all of them moved quietly. Although no order had been given it seemed they no longer had the common human habit of making noise. I guess that's what being a soldier does to you, thought Uno. Even if the war ends, we'll probably all tiptoe around for the rest of our lives, ready to dodge bullets or shoot at anyone who makes a threatening move.

After a very short time Mendoza ordered that the fire be put out and all of the men get to their hammocks to sleep, saving only the guards, who would be changed at two-hour intervals. Lolo, Juan, and one regular soldier drew first watch but Uno – enjoying no feeling of privilege – was allowed to tuck the baby into his own hammock under the one thin blanket, curl around him as best he could, and settle down for the night. Before the fire was extinguished, Mendoza gave them all a long silent look, pointed at the girl, and then gestured as if with a knife across his throat. They understood.

But as tired as he was, Uno found that he hung for a while in a twitching half-sleep. He kept seeing the awful scene of the village and the murdered people as if it had been stamped inside his head. He wondered if the others saw it too. But maybe Olivares, García, Captain Mendoza had seen it so often that it no longer haunted them. Yes, Olivares said he had, and that he grieved inside himself. But how much grief could a man stand? How many murdered babies could you look at and not go crazy? And then, lying there in the tropical darkness as thick as fog, he began to see that a man could go crazy, but he could do something else too. He could hate.

And that's what I'll do, he told himself. I'll hate them. Before, at home, I didn't see much difference between them – the loyalists and the revolutionaries. But now I do. And I've started hating the loyalists, and I'll always hate them.

And for some reason, this thought made him feel better. There, he thought as the outlines of the day grew fuzzy and murky and sleep at last crept closer, there . . . I won't go crazy. I'll just hate . . . them . . .

The baby cried once during the night. Uno awoke wondering what to do. While he struggled out of the hammock he heard a stir across the clearing and a grunt as Olivares also pulled himself out of his blanket. Together they fumbled the baby out of his wet wrapping and into a scrap of dry cloth, and Olivares opened a fresh tin of milk and put it into a cup with some water. As he tore a piece of cloth for the baby to suck on, he said, "Be careful. Don't let him choke."

Uno sat huddled in the darkness, feeling the jungle around him like a mold on his clothes, and wondered how it was possible that anyone thought they could keep the baby alive. "Olivares – he needs his mother –"

"We buried her."

"A bed – clean clothes – even dirty clothes would be better than no clothes at all –"

"Yes. But this is all we have now. Tomorrow –"

Uno felt the almost imperceptible weight of the child –

maybe four pounds – on his arm. "By tomorrow he'll have diarrhea. By tomorrow night he'll be dead."

"By tomorrow we can get him to the American mission. They have a doctor. And an orphanage," said Olivares quietly.

Uno's head jerked up. He strained to see Olivares's face, but the darkness was like a solid thing between them. "An American mission?" he whispered. "Here – in our country? Where?"

Olivares spoke so softly his voice was hardly more than a vibration between them. "Do not talk about it – not at all. The mission is not far away. We will leave the girl and the baby there. Say *nothing*."

There was a faint scuffle, and Uno knew Olivares had returned to his own hammock. He sat still while the infant sucked on the rag. The child was weak; Uno tipped the cup from time to time, letting extra milk run down into his mouth. Some of it was swallowed, more was wasted. Uno could only work by feel, and he knew the child could not live long on what few drops of milk he got.

But – a mission! A doctor! It was like living in purgatory all your life and suddenly learning that the door to heaven had been only a short distance away all the time. Why didn't we hear about this? he wondered urgently. Even Ignacio doesn't know there is a mission in this part of the country. Then he wondered why Olivares had told him not to speak about the mission. But of course – very quickly he realized that if people knew there was a mission – help of any kind – they would have been drawn to it like animals caught in a flood are drawn to a floating log. Sick, hungry, desperate, they would have crowded around it in such numbers that what help it might have offered would have been obliterated.

And beyond that, he knew something else now; a mission — many missions — could not save all the people of the country. Not even a few of them. And he wished he knew what *would* save them.

DAY FIVE

At daybreak they broke camp. Uno fed the baby again, and again it was difficult to get much into him. The girl was weak and feverish too.

They ate a cold meal, drank water from the canteens, and loaded up the heavy packs once more. Uno carried the baby, two rifles, and his blanket, into which had been rolled several packages of dry rations and a share of the ammunition. Once again his knees ached and his feet sank into the mud at every step. Before long the sweat streaming down his face blinded him and he was panting till his chest ached. Captain Mendoza, Olivares, García, Ignacio, and a couple of the others took turns with the stretcher. Before long Uno began to see black looks directed at Captain Mendoza's back as the stretcher bearers labored through the tangled undergrowth of the jungle.

At midmorning Mendoza called a halt. He directed Ignacio and Juan to make a clear spot, search for snakes, and arrange the equipment, station men at intervals on the perimeter for guards. Ignacio worked fast, but Juan was faster. No matter what he did, Uno thought sourly, Juan had to do it better and faster than anyone else. If he caught diarrhea, no doubt he would do that better and faster too.

When they were settled, Mendoza handed a canteen to Olivares and another to Uno. "Leave all your equipment here except your rifles – loaded" – he told them. "And a machete. Ramírez, you bring the child. Olivares and I will carry the stretcher."

As some minor shuffling was done Olivares glanced meaningfully at Uno. Uno said nothing.

"Olivares and Ramírez and I are going to take the girl and the baby to a village nearby where they will be cared for." As Mendoza spoke, he looked quietly from face to face. No one said anything, not a single face showed a question inside. "García will be in charge here. Rest as much as you can. We will be back in about two hours."

The captain and Olivares picked up the stretcher and plunged into the jungle. Uno, carrying the baby and all three of the rifles, followed. He glanced one last time at Lolo and Ignacio, they nodded gravely, and he nodded back.

He had wondered how the three of them, burdened as they were, could possibly fight their way through the jungle for two hours. It quickly developed that they would not have to.

In less than an hour they broke out of the heavy jungle onto a narrow track that led between ancient, tangled, vine-clad trees like a waterway through a canyon. Uno, walking now in the fore, felt waves of relief break over him as his back straightened and his legs pumped strong forward strides on the well-trodden path.

"Quickly! Faster!" ordered Mendoza behind him.

Uno shifted almost to a dogtrot, rounded a sharp bend in the trail, and skidded to a sudden halt.

Before them lay a tiny clearing centered by a tin-roofed house. Beside the house stood some kind of small truck, and in the doorway of the house was a woman.

Uno whirled in alarm, but behind him Mendoza and Olivares pressed forward, passed him, and hurried toward the woman in the doorway. Uno hastened after them. This must be the mission that Olivares had told him about.

Beside the house Mendoza and Olivares halted. They lowered the stretcher to the ground just as the woman approached on one side and Uno on the other.

"Mrs. Carter, we have two refugees for you," said Mendoza. "A girl – wounded – and a newborn child. They are both greatly in need of help. Can you take them?"

The woman – about twenty years old, Uno thought, and clad in blue jeans and a cotton shirt – bent over the girl on the stretcher. Her short blond hair glinted in the sun above her sun-reddened cheeks and blue eyes, and Uno suddenly realized that this was the first person he had ever seen with blond hair and blue eyes. Until this moment the world had been occupied only by people who had black hair and brown eyes. The woman looked strange – almost bleached, like bones whitened by the sun.

"Deep wound – infected." The woman spoke in badly accented Spanish. "Is it a bullet wound?"

"Yes. We had only some antiseptic."

"We shall do what we can. And you said also an infant?"

At this Uno stepped forward, directly facing and within a

breath's distance from the blond woman. She smelled good, although her fair skin was still shocking. He held out the child.

The woman took the baby. Her face was grave. She placed a finger on his throat. The child made a faint whisper of a cry.

"He is alive," said Uno.

The woman nodded. "Their names? Where are they from?"

Mendoza shook his head. "I don't know the name of their village, and they are the only survivors. Loyalists killed the rest. The girl's name is Magdalena Sánchez and the baby's name is Manolete. He is her brother, born yesterday. The girl may be able to tell you more. If she lives."

"She will live."

For a moment more they all stood there. There was so much they all could have said, Uno thought, that there was no use even to begin. None of them had time to talk about war and starvation and wounded children. What surprised him most was how empty his left arm suddenly felt. Then he stepped forward and reached out to smooth one finger over the baby's head. As he did so, he raised his eyes to the woman. All at once she smiled, and her blue eyes looked no longer strange, but familiar, like the sky above his own village. She raised a hand and touched her fingers gently to his arm. "Peace," she said.

Uno smiled too as he stepped back.

Mendoza nodded briskly. "Then we will go. Thank you, Mrs. Carter." He turned and Olivares and Uno turned also. But as Mendoza and Olivares plunged back down the trail, their feet hardly making a sound, Uno glanced back one more time at the mission. Two men had now appeared, and they were carrying the girl into the building. Mrs. Carter followed them, her yellow head bent over the baby.

"Go with God, little brother," whispered Uno. "Go with God."

They were back with the rest of the company in under an hour. Mendoza gave them a short rest, and Uno and Olivares were allowed a drink of water. Packs and rifles were redistributed, and now Uno too carried three guns and several rounds of ammunition as well as two canteens and his own pack. Juan, as always, carried a load as heavy as that borne by any of the older men. Then they were on their feet and slogging through the jungle again.

For two hours they followed Mendoza through the nearly impassable terrain, alternately cursing him when he couldn't hear them and cursing the mud and the jungle when he could.

Then, seconds after a troop of howler monkeys streamed by overhead, Mendoza suddenly flattened them to the ground with a hand signal. They sank into the cover of ferns and vines, and not one rifle clicked against a canteen, not one bundle of blanket-wrapped ammunition thumped as it hit the ground.

Uno kept even his breathing silent as all of them listened and watched. What had Captain Mendoza seen to give the alarm?

Then Ignacio passed a signal forward. "Captain – to the right – loyalists –"

"Yes."

Uno saw nothing, heard nothing but the beat of his own heart. Then – a few meters away – he caught a glimpse of a column of men – gray uniforms – straggling in loose order through the jungle. He saw a couple of orange shoulder patches; all the men carried rifles, and two carried rocket launchers. They seemed relaxed, not on guard, and were talking carelessly among themselves.

Uno had seen loyalists before – self-assured, well fed, arrogant men in clean uniforms and shiny black leather belts and boots – when they came through the village. In those days he and Lolo had tried to think of some way to steal a pair of their boots. Today he thought of something else: Are these the bastards who killed the villagers? No – Díaz wiped them all out. But they *are* loyalists. They will rape and murder some other village – maybe my own. We've got to kill them – kill them now – kill them –

From Mendoza, at the right end of their concealed line, came a whispered command: "Hold your fire till they are abreast of us. Wait for my signal – then fire at the man directly in front of you."

Uno inched his rifle up and slowly, slowly rolled over so he could get his legs out behind him. Shoot, he told himself. This is it. I am going to shoot, I am going to kill one of the bastards. He looked down at his gun. He had forgotten where the trigger was.

The loyalists were close now, not fifteen meters away. They moved as Mendoza's troop had been moving at an angle in such a way that the two lines of men would be opposite each other in a few more seconds. Now Uno could see their faces. This man had a crooked back, that one a pockmarked face. Another had a big nose – he looked like old Señor Calderon.

Now the man with the big nose was opposite Uno – he would have to shoot him –

Shots broke out. The sound cracked against Uno's ears.

At the last second he shut his eyes – can I shoot a man who looks like Señor Calderon? – and squeezed the trigger –

And raised the gun barrel.

So he would miss.

I couldn't, he cried inside his head. Oh, God, I couldn't do it. I couldn't shoot the man with a big nose –

Uno sat sullenly beside his pack and rifle as Lolo, next to him, pulled on a pair of black leather boots.

"Look!" cried Lolo exultantly. "Look! Look at that shine – that leather! Look!" He sprang to his feet and bent over to admire his feet encased in a pair of gleaming black boots which reached to the calves of his legs. They appeared to stick out somewhat farther than his bare toes would have, and the laces had to be drawn so tight the two sides met, but Lolo admiringly raised first one foot and then the other so he could see them better. "Leather boots! Real leather boots!" he said again. "I never had leather boots like these before!"

"You never had *any* boots before," said Uno sourly. "You never had anything but sandals or bare feet, like all the rest of us."

"I know – so –"

"So now you shot a man and you get to wear his boots."

"He was a loyalist bastard –"

"You shot him –"

Lolo stood up straight. "Listen, Uno, you'd better not talk like that. If Mendoza hears you –"

"Mendoza won't . . . say anything." But Uno squinted across the clearing at Mendoza. The captain seemed absorbed in his examination of the two captured rocket launchers and the rifles.

"How about Juan?" Lolo spoke very quietly, but even so a faint chill went over Uno. Both of them knew that if Juan heard Uno criticizing the killing of a loyalist soldier, Uno was going to find himself in real danger.

Uno was silent then, but he would not look at Lolo's boots. He stared at Ignacio who, with Juan, was now examining one of the rocket launchers.

"You ought to see if you can get some boots," urged Lolo. "Or a belt. Knife, machete, anything. This is war, Uno. If they had killed us they would have done the same."

Uno looked up through the tangled stems of the vines between them and the place where the bodies of the loyalists now lay. Their sprawled forms were just visible, and the scene brought back the horror of the village –

"I know. I know." He stared glumly at Lolo's new boots. He knew that it was customary for soldiers to do this. But it was not customary to see Lolo prancing around in shiny black boots. "Well, my feet aren't used to boots. They'd feel queer."

But the truth – the rock-bottom truth – was that Uno knew he had not earned the right to take any boots. He knew, as no one else did, that at the last moment he had been too weak to kill the man in front of his gun. Too weak. Too gutless. I thought I hated them, he told himself, after seeing what they did to the village. But then when it came to pulling the trigger – blowing the bastard's head off – I couldn't do it.

But he had no intention of telling Lolo he had shot to miss. Even if he faced the truth himself, Lolo would never understand it.

"Well, I've got a pair of boots now and I aim to keep them," said Lolo. "I feel like a man in boots."

"You look like a *cortero* in somebody else's clothes," said Uno, but he smiled.

Lolo snorted. "I am. I *am!*"

Lolo drifted away then to join Juan and the others around the rocket launchers. Uno stared drearily after him. War, he thought. Revolution. Captain Mendoza says we're out here building a whole new nation so everybody can be rich and happy. And Lolo, my friend, Lolo, who is closer to me than my own family – he kills a man so he can have his boots. That's what bandits do – kill a man for a pair of boots –

But, no . . . it wasn't that simple, he told himself honestly. Of course Lolo didn't kill the loyalist soldier in order to steal his boots. He killed the loyalist soldier because he had been conscripted into the revolutionary army which handed him a gun and ordered him to shoot. The revolutionists say they aim to make a better way of life for all the people – people like the dead villagers, the girl and the baby, even kids like Lolo and Ignacio and me. Lolo believes them now – yes, he does. And maybe Ignacio too. But me – what can I say? Yes, now that I've seen the village, I guess I believe it too. Some of it. But even though I believe it I couldn't shoot the loyalist in front of my gun. I couldn't.

"Uno!" He looked around. Lolo was beckoning. He drifted over to the others.

Captain Mendoza was speaking, his voice barely above a whisper. He and García had a piece of paper – part of a newspaper – which had evidently been taken off the body of one of the loyalists. He was reading scattered phrases. "It's from an underground newspaper, printed in Mexico City. It says that there are American mercenaries fighting here – with us – for the revolution. Maybe as many as thirty or forty men are here. Experienced combat veterans – probably men who served in Vietnam."

Olivares spoke. "Have you seen any of them, Captain?"

Mendoza shook his head. "No. But I have heard they were here. I believe they may be in General Godoy's units."

"Americans! Will they bring their own arms – ?"

"Jeeps? Tanks? Artillery?" Voices broke out all around.

"Helicopters?"

Mendoza rose quickly. "Quiet. The Americans – wherever they are – are mercenaries. That means they are not using American equipment nor operating out of American ports or airfields. They will be on about the same footing we are. So don't expect the war to end tomorrow. Forty – or one hundred and forty – men will help, but they won't win the war for us." Crisply Mendoza motioned for García and Olivares to get ready to move out. "Load up. We'll have to carry the extra arms and ammunition again. It will be hard going – we'll have rest stops every half-hour."

"Captain – shall we bury them?" Olivares nodded at the bodies of the loyalists.

"No time. We've been here too long now," said Mendoza. "I want to get back to the fortress by nightfall."

Uno stood like a donkey and stared at the load of rifles, supplies, and ammunition that García handed out to each man. I should have grabbed some of those boots after all, he told himself. Then when I dropped dead of exhaustion I would make a very well-dressed corpse. Not to mention that then somebody else could steal them from me.

After leaving the place where they had ambushed the loyalists they turned northeastward and began working their way up out of the jungle lowlands and into the mountains. In the late afternoon, they came onto a road that wound upward through groves of pines and patches of open grassland.

At the moment when Uno felt he would finally and utterly collapse, Mendoza called a halt and he dropped his burden to the ground. They fell in the dust where they stood.

Then, through a haze of sweat and exhaustion, Uno saw Mendoza signal to someone ahead on the road. As he watched, a small party of men appeared. They were *corteros*, peons, like himself and the others, not in uniform but in ragged civilian clothes. At their head was a man who looked so much like a bandit he would have to be one. He wore crossed bandoleers and a huge pistol on his hip, and he had a long mustache and a wide-brimmed straw hat.

Mendoza saluted and greeted the leader. "Choya. I'm glad to see you."

Choya nodded and grunted. He didn't seem all that glad to see Mendoza and his soldiers, but rather gave the impression of having kept a business appointment of some kind.

Mendoza gestured wearily back at his exhausted men. Uno, Lolo, and Ignacio glanced questioningly at each other, but Juan appeared to know what to expect. He started unloading his pack and sorting out the extra rifles he carried. The others followed.

The *corteros* moved quickly down the line gathering up packs, equipment, the extra rifles, and boxes of ammunition. They loaded the heavy burdens on their backs until they looked like mechanical objects with lumps and packs and gun barrels sticking out all over. As soon as they were loaded they started on up the road, each man bearing an impossible weight.

Choya stood talking to Mendoza. "Twenty-five rifles," he said, "and ammunition." He was a powerful man, short but strong. Nothing in his manner seemed easy, cooperative, or even civil.

"Ten rifles," Mendoza replied, "and ammunition. Two machetes."

"Laughable." Choya took something out of his pocket and blew on it. There was a short whistle, like the sound of a bird, and instantly the line of burdened men halted.

"Twenty-three rifles," said Choya. "Ammunition and six machetes."

Uno leaned toward Juan. "What are they doing? Who are they?" he whispered.

"Quiet. It's Choya. His band helps carry freight for us. Sometimes they bring in supplies. Captain Mendoza has to pay him. They are bargaining."

Uno stared at the peasants, at Choya. "But – they are just like us. They live here. The revolution is for them – why don't they –"

"Work for nothing?" Juan turned to stare at Uno, and Uno thought if ever there were a soldier's face – committed, unswerving – it was Juan's. "No. We have to pay him. A lot."

"*Money?*"

"No – guns."

"But those are army rifles. What does he do with them?"

"Sells them."

Uno watched Juan's face carefully. He wasn't sure he wanted to ask this. "Sells them . . . to whom?"

Juan seemed all at once to crawl inside himself. "To loyalists. To . . . us."

"But . . . he is . . . one of *us* –"

Juan leaned forward. "Shut up. Captain Mendoza will hear you. Choya will hear you. This is the way it is. This is the way we fight this war. Alone. Sometimes the people we fight for aren't even with us. And sometimes the people we fight against aren't always *against* us. You don't always know if someone is your enemy or your friend. So it pays to be careful of everybody. You stay alive longer. Just remember – we fight alone. If we win, the people will love us. Some of them. If we lose, they will hate us. Some of them. Nothing is ever easy in this war or in this country. But *they* are the people – *we* are the army. And all we have is each other. Remember that."

At the head of the line there was a stir of completed bargaining.

"Eighteen rifles," said Mendoza. "No more."

"Done." The bird whistle sounded. Choya and his line of men moved off.

All we have is each other. All we have is each other. Juan's words repeated in his mind like a drumbeat. Although they had only to walk – not march – it seemed that all their feet struck the ground in rhythm with the words "All we have is each other."

Is he right? Uno asked himself. And the answer came up from somewhere deep inside him – yes, he is. And he also knew, staggering up the dark road after this violent day, that in some way he had ceased to be one of the "people" and had become one of the "patrol." The patrol had been a terrible experience with two separate kinds of people. The villagers who were murdered – they were one kind of people. His patrol had dealt with the murderers – the patrol was another kind of people. But even though he had been unable to kill the loyalist soldier in front of his gun, he knew at last that it was to the patrol that he now belonged. It was not because he wanted to be here – he didn't – but that had nothing to do with it. But because he and the others on the patrol had marched, eaten, sweated, been angry and grieving and scared, and had done something terrible and impossible together, they had become "the patrol." And would always be. Like lumps of metal heated over a fire that run together to make a solid whole, the day had taken them and melted them into a whole. He did not know how it had happened, but he knew that it had.

I will always remember this day, he told himself. Nothing

will ever be the same again. *I* will never be the same person I was before I came to the fortress . . . before the patrol . . .

Darkness was falling quickly now, and the road rose steeply. Uno knew they must be nearing the fortress on a different road from the one on which they had left. Even with the relief from the burden of the extra rifles, ammunition, and supplies, they were all dead tired. Beyond tired, thought Uno, watching the heels of the man ahead of him, Juan, as he dragged one foot after the other. None of us is really awake. What if a loyalist patrol jumps us? But the forest was silent and empty.

It was almost full dark when they reached the fortress; Uno was barely aware of the fact that the road they were on had merged with the one they came out on. They began to encounter sentries two kilometers out, then every two or three hundred meters. Uno hoped the sentries were alert; he didn't want to get shot by men who were on his side in the war.

Then Díaz called out, "Halt!" And there was a bumpy sound of gates opening. Small lights appeared — flashlights — that stabbed here and there, and as Díaz ordered them forward through the gate, each man was carefully scrutinized. The lights blinded them and they bumped into each other as they passed through. There were a few tired curses, but for the most part they simply stumbled forward.

Then they rounded a cluster of pine trees and there was the Headquarters tent; a pair of propane lanterns, and men waiting with hot food.

From brutal experience they had learned not to bolt. Rifles

were stacked, packs laid down, ammunition surrendered. Then they shuffled forward to receive their food.

Uno was almost too tired to care. Even though he was ravenously hungry, he accepted his plate and cup in silence.

In order not to blunder around in the dark the men of the patrol gathered to one side of the lantern-lit space, crumpled to the ground, and began to eat.

As he ate, the hot food and the coffee began to make Uno feel better. He noted that the others did too. Backs straightened, chins lifted off chests, voices, though weary, were a little stronger, more confident. After eating, Mendoza and Díaz disappeared into the Headquarters tent. Uno yawned, coughed, yawned again.

Beside him Lolo groaned faintly. He set his empty plate down and began to slowly ease his boots off. His face was pale and strained. There was a sucking sound as the first boot came off – along with bits of skin from the blisters it had worn. Uno stared at Lolo's foot. It was bleeding. Lolo pulled the other boot off. The other foot was as bad as the first.

"You stupid fool!" hissed Uno. "Look what you've done! You had to wear those damned boots! Now you'll die of gangrene!" He glanced at his own feet – thin, bony, brown, and – God! so tired – but sound and unblemished in his rope sandals.

Lolo sat in silence. He was past saying anything.

Juan turned and saw Lolo's feet. "God," he said with a disgusted look, and rose to his feet. As he strode toward the Headquarters tent they heard him say, "Crazy, stupid bastard! Captain Mendoza, sir, we have a casualty –"

Ignacio crawled over to look at Lolo's feet. "Lolo, why did you keep them on? You must have known better."

Lolo finally spoke. "I didn't . . . want to lose them."

Uno groaned. "Now you may lose your feet."

Ignacio peeled his shirt off and lay it on the ground. "Put your feet on this, so they won't be in the dirt. If they have any antibiotics here you'll be all right."

"What's an an – ti – ?"

"Medicine that stops infection. Here comes Juan."

Uno and Ignacio made themselves utterly silent as Juan, followed by Captain Mendoza and Sergeant Batista, approached.

Captain Mendoza halted, leaned over to look at Lolo's feet. He glared at Lolo. "Have I lost a good soldier because you were so stupid you got blisters on your feet?"

Lolo, who had evidently been planning to either excuse himself or ask for help, snapped his mouth shut. Then, placing his wounded feet on Ignacio's shirt, he shakily stood up. "No, sir," he whispered. And then again, "*No – sir!*"

Mendoza stared at him. "This time, you're lucky. We have medicine. Fortunately you made a good showing on patrol, and I will have you taken to the Headquarters tent for medical treatment. But we do not have medicine for fools who hurt themselves. Only for combat wounds. Remember that. Sergeant, get him to the tent."

Batista stepped forward, turned to two men standing nearby, and made a signal. The two men made a sling of their arms, scooped Lolo into it, and in a moment they had carried him off into the darkness. Batista followed.

Mendoza kicked the boots. "Boots," he said angrily. "We are fighting a war and it comes down to this – we nearly lost a man who blistered his own feet."

All were silent.

Then Uno – too tired to care about safety or discipline and watching his closest friend disappear – said, "Captain – sir – you said he was – a good soldier?"

Mendoza stood for a moment longer. Then he said, "Yes. He did well. All of you . . . did well." He paused to give Uno a level look, and Uno had a sudden flash of understanding that the captain knew exactly how much and when and where he had fallen short on the patrol. He wondered desperately why he was not being punished and why the captain said, "All of you . . . did well."

"Next time," said Mendoza as he turned away, "you will do better."

In a short time Lolo returned from the Headquarters tent. He was on his feet, though hobbling, with white bandages wrapped up to his ankles. He wore a pair of pale blue canvas shoes with the word NIKE printed on them. Uno wanted to see the shoes up close but decided to wait till morning. Lolo didn't look as if he were in any mood to show off his new footgear. And Uno also noticed that he picked up his stolen boots and rammed them defiantly under his arm as if to prevent their being grabbed off by anyone else. Then at a sign from Díaz they all gathered up their blankets from where they had been dropped (by Choya's donkeys) and staggered off to their sleeping place.

As he stumbled away into the darkness, Uno found he was remembering the captain's words. He said we did well. We buried some people, saved two children, killed some loyalists. Thinking back, it seemed to him that the losses on the patrol had been enormous – the people they were too late to rescue, even the guns with which they had to "pay" Choya. Maybe that's what a war is – some losses, some gains, he thought. But Mendoza said we did well . . .

When he rolled into his blanket Uno looked up once and saw a blur of stars, then he simply sank under the weight of his fatigue into a bottomless, dreamless place where nothing – not even himself – existed.

DAY SIX

The whistle sounded at daybreak, but Uno did not hear it. None of the men who had been on patrol heard it; all slept as if dead for another hour. Then Sergeant Díaz visited each of them personally and kicked him sharply in the ribs.

"Up," he said. "Up. Out. You've had an extra hour's sleep. Up. The war goes on."

Uno's eyes opened, and he stared at the horizon of grass ten inches from his face. He wondered if it would be possible to assassinate Díaz, along with Juan and Esteban and Whistler, during the next battle. He mentioned this idea quietly to Lolo as the two of them crept out of their blankets and staggered to their feet.

"Why not kill Mendoza too?" suggested Lolo. "He's the one who brought us here."

But Uno did not want to kill Mendoza, even though Lolo was right. As he shook and rolled his blanket he wondered why. At last he said, "No. There's something about Mendoza. I don't know what it is. Yes, I do. It's – he's –"

Lolo felt his feet through the canvas shoes. He winced.

"Sure. You know all about Mendoza."

"He's —" Again Uno had to stop. He knew that he had a powerful feeling about Mendoza — he suspected that the other men had it also — but for the moment he could not find words to describe the feeling.

Nacio, now awake too, and on his feet, supplied them. "He's a leader."

For a moment they considered this.

Then, "Sure," said Lolo. "He led us right to that village — *after* the loyalists killed all the people." He took his blanket and rolled the boots in it and placed the bundle far back under a bush.

Uno stared down the slope at the burial ground and remembered all those graves in the village. Only two children had escaped. "He didn't kill them. The loyalists did that —"

Lolo went on. "And then he led us back to the fortress and my feet had no skin on them when we got here."

"That was your own damn fault," said Nacio bluntly. "You had to dress up in somebody else's boots, so you blistered your feet. How are they, by the way?"

Lolo looked thoughtful. "Sore. But I don't suppose I'll get out of drill."

"You're just lucky they had medicine and bandages for you — and a doctor," said Uno grudgingly, but neither he nor Nacio objected when Lolo pushed their blanket rolls under the bush to help conceal his own bundle containing the boots.

"They don't have a doctor," said Lolo. He got to his feet, his face twitching, and then limped heavily off toward the mess tent, where they could see men lining up for coffee.

"Then who bandaged your feet?" Uno called after him.

And barely heard the answer that Lolo tossed back over his shoulder: "Mendoza."

They drilled for three hours, maybe more. It was jungle practice again – creep, hide, advance, attack, fall back, hide, advance again. Uno was sure that if Atlacatl had erupted during drill Juan would not have swerved or slowed down until molten lava was lapping at his feet. *His* feet, not theirs.

Shortly after noon they were ordered back to the Headquarters area where a meal was waiting for them. This time there was stewed chicken meat tossed over the rice, and they were allowed two cups of coffee. Uno ate his chicken first. If the war, the volcano, or Juan happened to blow up just now, he wanted to die with meat in his stomach.

After they finished eating, piled the tin plates in the basket, and were given the second cup of coffee, they retired to the shade of their favorite tree and settled for a short rest.

"Wish I had a cigarette," said Lolo.

"I couldn't steal any more," said Nacio regretfully. "And there's no place to buy any here – even if we had some money."

"What I'd like," said Lolo, staring out over the dusty, dun-colored camp, "is to go to the U.S. and get a good job and be able to buy cigarettes whenever I want to."

Uno glanced at him indifferently. He had heard Lolo say this before and knew he didn't mean it. There had been a man in the village – his name was Joaquín – who had made the trip to the United States, overland through Mexico, and after spending three or four years in and out of a place called Juarez, had come home. He said he had become a "wetback" and had gone across a river to look for work in the U.S. He and hundreds of others had drifted around, doing farm work here and there, sleeping in tents or on the bare dirt, eating no better than he had at home. The money he made, though certainly far more than he could have made in their village, or anywhere in the country, had only bought him a small field and a used plow. He planned to go north to the U.S. again so he could earn money to buy his own team of oxen, only he came down with tuberculosis and the last Uno had heard of him he would likely die before he could make such a pilgrimage again. Joaquín had told them that he was sure he caught tuberculosis from sleeping on the ground under a farm truck near a place called Stockton. Watching Joaquín stand and look at his useless field as his lungs came out of his mouth, one cough at a time, had not made any of them want to go to the U.S. and become wetbacks.

But it made you think . . .

"I wonder what it would be like to have a good job," said Uno. "Cigarettes. Chicken – once a week, maybe."

"Boots that fit." This from Lolo.

"Go to school – a university. *Be* somebody special," said Nacio. "Not just a damn *cortero* or *chiclero* and starve to death while the owner of the plantation drives by in his big fancy car –"

"– on his way to the harbor to take a ride on his boat –"

"– or to get in his airplane and fly around."

"Mendoza has an airplane." A shadow fell over them and they looked up. It was Juan. "Captain Mendoza has a little airplane of his own, and he flies from one camp to another. Sometimes he goes to the U.S. to see people. He borrows money from them for the revolution."

Uno, Lolo, and Nacio considered this. So far as they knew, Juan did not customarily lie. Of course, he didn't have to. He outranked them.

"So how did a captain in the revolutionary army get enough money to buy an airplane – if he did buy it?" asked Nacio.

Juan sipped his coffee. "I heard he took it out of a bank when the revolutionists captured a town north of here."

"That's stealing."

"That's revolution," said Juan flatly. "Where else would he get an airplane? And he uses it to help win the war."

"All the same . . ."

"All the same – what?" said Juan sharply. "That's how you win a revolution. You don't fight fair. You fight hard. To win."

"All the same . . . if one of us took money out of a bank we sure as hell wouldn't get away with spending it any way we wanted to. We couldn't even buy a pack of cigarettes," grunted Uno. He knew what Juan would do if he found out Nacio had stolen the cigarettes the other day and reminded himself never to tell Juan anything more than he had to. Juan was a soldier, and nothing else.

"Of course you wouldn't be allowed to do things like that," said Juan crisply. "Officers have privileges we don't have. If you don't like it, you have to try to become an officer."

"How does that change anything?" growled Nacio. "It's still stealing, isn't it?"

"Not when you're an officer," said Juan.

The whistle blew. "Drill," said Lolo as he carefully rose to his feet. "I've got to work hard – I'm going to be a captain some day – so I can have my own airplane –"

"Well, then you can wear boots and get blisters and it won't matter," said Uno.

During drill the rest of the afternoon, Uno found himself thinking, from time to time, about Captain Mendoza's airplane. He believed that Mendoza used it for the revolutionary cause – the captain would do that, he was sure – but what about the bank and the man in charge of it? What did he tell the people whose money was taken to buy the airplane? And how did they feel about having their money used to buy an airplane that, however else it was used, wasn't likely ever to fly back and return their money? Uno felt he was stranded, like a man crossing a swamp on hummocks of grass. On one side he saw the need for the airplane and on the other the needs of the people who put their money into the bank. You had to do a very fancy balancing act, he decided at last, to steer between the needs of those two opposing sides and not fall into the swamp.

It was some time before it occurred to him that Mendoza, on the patrol, had walked just as far as everybody else had, airplane or no airplane.

And for some reason that made him feel better.

Late in the day there was another meal, not so sumptuous as the earlier one, but it filled them up, and Uno wondered if there might be a chance to play baseball before it got dark. He finally mentioned this to Juan, but for once Juan seemed too distracted to snap back an angry answer.

"No. There's talk about a big move. We've received messages over the radio that the loyalists are moving on San Ildefonso and unless the other guerrilla units there can turn them back we may have to cross the river tomorrow and support them." Juan's voice was crisp, detached, businesslike.

Uno stared at him. What was it that made Juan – only two years older than himself – so different? Juan, he had already acknowledged, was all soldier, with a sharp commanding manner and a sense of weight about him that set him apart even from soldiers older than himself. Uno had started off automatically hating him because Juan was just one of his jailers. But even while he was busy hating him, Uno knew he was burning and itching to outdo Juan some way. Juan was so damned right about whatever he did. He didn't stumble, fumble, forget, or mess up – never. Grimly Uno realized that, whether he wanted to be here in this revolutionary army or not, what he did want – and must do – was find some way to beat Juan –any way he could do it.

Nothing else would ever satisfy him.

DAY SEVEN

He woke at daybreak. Birds were singing, and a light wind was fluffing through the tops of the trees. Quietly he turned his head. Nacio, Lolo, and some others he knew by name and some he did not lay scattered here and there, all still asleep. Their stillness made him think about the bodies of the loyalist soldiers left in the jungle. His companions looked no more alive than they did.

He pulled himself out of the blanket just as the whistle blew. He poked a rough fist at Lolo and Ignacio, and they raised their heads to stare bleary-eyed out at the camp. One by one each of them staggered to his feet, brushed back his hair, and kicked his blanket into a pile back under the brush and out of the way. Lolo was still limping badly, and the blue canvas shoes looked exotic on his feet.

They stumbled through the lines at the latrines and then, seeing that coffee was being handed out, went to stand in that line. Although men all around him were talking quietly Uno was silent. Neither Lolo nor Nacio said anything until they all had tin cups of hot coffee. Then they shuffled off to their customary spot, sat down, and each one took several swallows from his cup.

"Christ," said Lolo, "you'd think we could sleep late once in a while."

"Where do you think you are?" grunted Nacio. "At a fiesta? This is war."

"I keep forgetting," said Lolo. "I've hardly killed more than half a dozen men."

"Half a dozen?" scoffed Nacio. "You might have chipped a front tooth on one loyalist bastard. I saw you firing. What makes you think you hit anybody? You're supposed to brace yourself – watch your balance – get a grip on your rifle –"

"I suppose you did better? How many did you kill?"

Uno listened to the low-level rumble of their bickering and knew they were warmly complimenting each other on a job well done. He wished he could join the conversation, but he couldn't. Even though, last night, he had realized he had finally become one of the patrol, still he had not shot anybody. He knew – as Lolo and Nacio did not – that at the moment of truth he had not been able to shoot the man with the big nose. Somebody else had.

They brought me out here to make a soldier of me, and all I did was go on a long march, help bury some dead people, and carry a baby to someone who will try to keep him alive for a few more days. And as he sat there nursing his coffee and feeling the warmth of it building in his belly, his thought grew stronger and stronger and turned into a voice and he heard himself say out loud, "It's not enough. It's not enough."

Lolo and Ignacio turned. "What isn't enough?" asked Lolo blankly.

Uno looked around in confusion. "Oh . . . nothing. I wasn't thinking."

"Well, I wasn't thinking either when I put those boots on," admitted Lolo with deep regret.

"Can you walk better now?" Ignacio leaned over to inspect the bandages sticking out above the shoes.

"Oh, yes. I can walk. I *have* to walk."

A shadow fell across their faces, and they looked up. It was Juan. Whistler was just behind him. They had coffee, and Whistler was lighting a cigarette.

"Well, soldier, how are your pretty feet this morning?" asked Juan pleasantly. "Do you plan to fight the rest of this war in those ballet slippers?"

Lolo glared at him. "I kept up," he said furiously. "I *will* keep up. You'll see –"

"Crap. Get your rifles. Díaz is going to drill us this morning. *If* you can make it –"

Juan turned away to summon others, but Whistler lingered another moment. He directed a contemptuous look at Uno. "The little mother," he said. "Carried a stinking brat all the way through the jungle so others had to carry the real loads – rifles, ammunition."

"Captain Mendoza – I had orders!" cried Uno sharply. "What else could I –"

"What else? I'll tell you what else. *I* would have strangled the bastard on the way and told the captain it died. All you did was save one more useless mouth to feed. We can't fight a revolution and play mommy to a bunch of crying babies. It takes all the food – all the strength – all the guts we have just to fight. There's no place here for babies." He turned on his heel and followed Juan.

Uno stared thoughtfully after him. "Lolo," he said at last, "If there's ever any chance of my having to fall into Whistler's . . . care . . . I want you to shoot me first. *Por favor*."

Lolo nodded. "Makes you hope Mendoza doesn't get shot."

A whistle blasted, and they started off toward it. "Yes," said Nacio, "I'm glad Mendoza is running this place. And I never thought I'd say that."

Morning drill lasted two hours. They ate, rested, and in the early afternoon they were again summoned by the whistle. They had been dozing in the shade, and it took them a few seconds to rouse themselves and brush the dust off their clothes. As they hurried back toward Headquarters Lolo looked around. "What's going on?" he muttered. "Look – they're loading the trucks. What's going on?"

Ignacio peered down the slope. "There are some different guns on that truck. They look like SAMs. I never saw them before. Where have they been?"

Uno looked across at the men scurrying around in front of Headquarters. Although there seemed to be a lot of confusion, in fact he could see that a great deal of work was being done. Several squads of men were loading supplies into trucks – rifles, crates, tools, cans of water and fuel drums, metal chests – probably ammunition – that had been stored around the fortress. Uno noted curiously that Captain Mendoza's battered wooden table stood in its usual place even though the Headquarters tent that stood behind it was being dismantled. The table was covered by a drift of papers, and several officers were clustered around it.

"*Adelante!*" snapped Juan as they approached. "Over there – help carry the blankets and medical supplies."

They hurried to the third tent. "Load these on truck thirty-seven!" said Juan sharply, nodding at rows of rolled-up hammocks, blankets, mess kits, and boxes marked with red crosses.

Uno, Lolo, and Nacio grabbed loads of blankets. As they staggered down the hill, Uno said, "Truck thirty-seven? Does that mean there are thirty-six other trucks here?"

"No," grunted Lolo. "I heard somebody say it means the loyalists blew up thirty-six other trucks and this is number thirty-seven. They'll blow it up too, as soon as they see it."

"I hope I'm not in it."

"You won't be." It was Juan, who now bobbed up beside the truck to direct the loading of the packs. "You won't be on any truck. You'll be on foot – marching."

As he thrust his load up onto the truck bed, Uno felt a chill creep over him. "March? How far?" he wanted to know. Could Lolo stand another march on his blistered feet?

"Not far," said Juan grimly as he slammed the rolled packs down to fit them in as tightly as possible. "You new men and Sergeant Díaz and some others will be sent down to hold the place on the Río Santiago where we will all have to cross tomorrow –"

"What do you mean 'we'?" cried Lolo. "Where will the rest of you be?"

"Regrouping. And I will be with the rocket crew. I'm to be

trained to handle a rocket launcher. You will hold the ford at the river, and then tomorrow –" He halted as the whistle sounded above them and a volley of orders cracked out.

"Yes – tomorrow?" asked Ignacio urgently. "What happens tomorrow?"

"San Ildefonso has fallen. The loyalists have taken it. Tomorrow we attack in force across the river and take it back. This is no patrol, babies. This will be a major battle. We'll draw blood this time, and no mistake."

Juan jumped down out of the truck and charged off, but Uno did not even see him go. At Juan's mention of "blood" he suddenly saw the murdered village again. How much blood, he wondered desperately, how much blood is it going to take to win this war?

"Jesus, Mary, Joseph – I hope we can do it," said Ignacio through clenched teeth. "How can we fight a big battle? We only just stopped falling over our rifles. Killing the loyalist patrol was just good luck. They happened to march right in front of us and all we had to do was shoot them down like target practice."

And I've never even shot my rifle *at* anyone, thought Uno. Whistler said it: I'm just a baby-sitter. But aloud he said, "I don't have any ammunition. Just the one bullet we have for drill."

"Maybe the loyalists only have one bullet apiece too," said Lolo grimly. "That ought to make it a short battle."

They carried load after load of blankets, food, water cans, until truck number thirty-seven was finally loaded. Then they were ordered back to the spot where they had been sworn in on the day they arrived. Captain Mendoza and others were still at the table, but they were rolling up the maps. And now at last a man grabbed up the table and hurried off to toss it up onto a truck.

Esteban appeared out of the crowd. "Get your rifles. And get back here fast!"

They ran to the tree where their rifles were stacked – Uno knew his by the mud on the barrel – and ran back to place.

"Fall in!"

They snapped into some kind of order, a straight line, straight backs, rifles shouldered, eyes ahead. Lolo's face was impassive, and Uno wondered how much his feet hurt. He had not limped once this morning.

Captain Mendoza walked out of the crowd and faced them. "At ease," he said crisply. "I expect you all have heard by now – San Ildefonso has fallen. We must take it back. Possession – or at least access to – San Ildefonso is absolutely necessary to us. If we don't have this, we have no chance at all. We are fighting a bloody, damned, uphill war so that some day the people of this country will have a chance to live and work in peace. But – you must understand – peace is very expensive. It costs a lot of money and a lot of blood. We can either go on starving as we have always done, or we can fight and try to make things better. For me –" he paused for only one second as he stared down the hill at the graves – "for me and my son the choice was and is to fight. I believe that together we can win the struggle and that life will some day be better for us all. And so for now – may God lead us to victory." He turned to the officers beside him. "Units A, C, D, and F will be transported by truck to the rear staging area for regrouping. Units B and E, under Lieutenant De Soto"

— he glanced directly at Sergeant Díaz — "and Sergeant Díaz, will march to the ford in the Río Santiago to hold it. There you will set up defensive positions and hold them till the rest of us are able to make the crossing in force. Then we will advance together and take back San Ildefonso." He paused, and just for one second Uno knew the captain's eyes flicked over his face. "Many of you are new men — have only just begun your training. I regret — I deeply regret the necessity of sending you into a major battle before you are — before you have had thorough training. I had not planned to do this, but events have forced us. We must take San Ildefonso back. If we fail, we will have more long years of struggle before we can win this revolution."

And Atlacatl will eat us up, thought Uno as he stood ramrod straight. He, Lolo, and Ignacio were in Unit E — as well as Juan and Esteban. They would be sent to hold the ford at the river.

Captain Mendoza drew himself up and saluted. Every man returned the salute.

As the captain turned to go, Uno stared after him. "I wish I could talk to him some more," he whispered. "There are things I want to ask him."

The road leading out of the fortress was rutted and dusty, and the men who had to march had bad footing. Uno had just decided it was as bad as the jungle when a command was passed back down the straggling lines to turn right off the road, angling off down the slope.

Before the trees closed behind them Uno jerked around

for one last look backward at the fortress. Funny, he thought. When I'm inside the fortress, it feels like a prison. But from out here, it's just a high fence around some trees and rocks. It occurred to him that it wasn't just the fence that made the fortress a fortress, but when he turned to mention this to Lolo and the others, he could see that their mood was hurried, harried, and he decided it wasn't important. What mattered, like a warning rumble from Atlacatl, was the coming battle.

Since there was no particular order to keep, the three boys walked close together. From habit Uno and Lolo walked shoulder to shoulder, with Ignacio, who was taller, a stride behind them. Esteban was behind Ignacio, silent as usual, and Juan was somewhere ahead.

Since instructions had been passed to be as quiet as possible, which meant no talking, Uno tried to occupy his mind by watching the other men, the trail, the surrounding country. It was really just their same old packing-shed habit of watch and watch out, transplanted to a mountainside and a war.

Uno noted that the column of men numbered about thirty, not including the lieutenant and sergeant, and all of them carried heavy packs. Sergeant Díaz marched at the head and Lieutenant De Soto at the rear. Uno was relieved to note that the majority of men, twenty or more, were older and more experienced fighters than himself. He worried, though, about the remaining third – himself, Lolo, Ignacio, and several other very young boys he had seen only briefly inside the fortress. He already recognized that he knew next to nothing about fighting, and except for those rare outbursts of talent like the time Lolo had jumped on his back, neither did most of the other new recruits. The patrol had taught him absolutely nothing about fighting except that he was a rotten soldier. What kind of a fight could they be expected to make?

Along with his own lack of ability, he quickly began to worry about the difficulty of the journey. For several hours they had been threading their way down an interlocking system of ravines until they were far below the open, cool pine groves. Now, on flat land, they were into forests of palm, bamboo, and strangler fig. Ferns and vines grabbed their feet, and clouds of black flies tormented them. But they had been told they were to hold a ford in the river – that meant they would be in jungle all the way to their objective. Uno swept a cloud of black flies from his face and promised himself that if God ever gave him a chance to leave this country, he would take it, and no questions asked. He thought longingly of smooth sidewalks and nice, clean brick buildings. Heaven, he told himself, must be a very long way from here and have streetlights and buses and clean, cold water running out of faucets.

And finally he began to be hungry again. Actually he hardly ever stopped being hungry, he just got more hungry sometimes and less at others. Just as the cramps in his belly began to make him feel like vomiting, there was a signal to halt.

Just ahead a shimmer of light through the trees marked the location of a clearing – perhaps a farm or a very small village.

"At ease. Rest your legs."

Tired as they were, they selected resting places carefully.

Snakes, insects, ants, spiders, certainly thorned plants were everywhere.

Lolo peered ahead. "Why are we stopping?"

The lieutenant silenced him with a look.

For several minutes nothing seemed to be happening, then finally they saw Sergeant Díaz stand up. He moved forward carefully. It appeared that he was signaling to someone they could not see. Presently a strange figure appeared. It was a man – a peasant – who approached carefully, one step at a time, till he was close enough to talk to Sergeant Díaz. Then he turned and vanished.

They sat on for several minutes, feeling some of the weary ache drain away to be replaced by mounting hunger and thirst.

"I'm hungry," mouthed Uno silently.

"Me too," nodded Lolo.

"Why – ?"

"Quiet!"

Then through the trees the peasant reappeared. He was followed by two other men and an old woman. All carried burdens of some kind wrapped in squares of cloth, and two had buckets.

When the peasants reached them they opened their bundles and quickly began to distribute the contents.

"Tortillas!" breathed Uno.

"Beans – melons –" whispered Lolo.

"Coffee," said Ignacio with a sigh as the buckets and some cups and drinking gourds were passed around.

The peasants worked fast. They moved through the men

and saw to it that each had a meal. Each man received enough, and not one bean or scrap of tortilla was wasted. The old woman even licked a splash of coffee off her wrist instead of wiping it on her skirt.

As he shoveled food into his mouth Uno could not look at the peasants. Hungry as he was, he suddenly knew he was eating the food that would have fed the peasants, probably for a week. "God, give them more," he prayed silently. "We have to have this food or we can't even march. But, God – give these people more so they won't go hungry –"

As the meal was finished and the peasants gathered up their empty cloths and the gourds and cups and disappeared like white shadows, his prayer turned into a kind of marching song. The men clambered to their feet, shouldered their rifles, and circled what they now saw was a tiny cluster of huts and gardens, and as they struck off at a slightly different angle, Uno heard a voice monotonously reciting in his head: "God, give them food. God, give us food. Why are we always so hungry? God, give them food. God, give us food. Why are we always so hungry – ?"

He could tell by the way the jungle thickened as they made their torturous way forward in a ragged line that they were nearing the river Captain Mendoza had spoken about. This would be the Río Santiago, a smaller river than the Santa María. The Santa María was a big, fat river that wound through the coastal lowlands, never far from the Caribbean shore, and this river, the Santiago, rose on the Pacific side of the mountain chain that ran north and south from border to border in the country, and carried less water, which emptied into a big lake south of San Ildefonso. No one would ever think of fording the Santa María, if for no other reason than the snakes and crocodiles that liked to laze in the shallows under the trees along the banks. But the Santiago could be forded in one or two places, even though the jungle on both sides made those fords hard to reach. Uno wished now that the jungle here was such that no army would be needed to guard this ford. But even though the ground was increasingly wet underfoot and the air heavy with moisture, and the light at ground level dim under a ceiling of treetops seventy to one hundred feet up, it was just possible to force one's way through it.

At last in the early evening a halt was called. Two men were detailed to search for snakes, and two more went behind them with machetes to clear some of the lower growth. A small clearing twenty feet or so in diameter was prepared, and in this they found or made places to sit. The packs borne by the older men were opened and their very scant supplies revealed. Uno and the others watched as several thin blankets and cord hammocks were unloaded. There were some plastic-wrapped bundles that contained simple medical equipment and a few heavy metal boxes that were piled in the center of the clearing and guarded carefully by two men.

"Ammunition." Lolo formed the word soundlessly.

Uno nodded. "I wonder how close we are to the river."

Díaz, passing by, said, "Twenty, maybe thirty meters."

Lieutenant De Soto now produced a small metal can and some bits of cloth. "Clean your rifles," he said as he distributed the shreds of cotton fabric.

The can was passed around, and each man dabbed some liquid on his cleaning cloth. Uno took his and scrubbed at the mud and dust caked on his gun. Cleaning rods, which were attached to each rifle, were used to remove any grit from inside the barrels.

When all the rifles had been cleaned De Soto stood up. "Distribute the ammunition," he directed.

Sergeant Díaz squatted down and opened one of the metal chests. They watched silently as clips were removed and handed around. Uno took his and loaded his rifle. He hefted the gun and felt the difference in its weight and balance.

"Do *not* release the safeties," said the lieutenant. "Safeties are to be off only when you are in position and ready to fire. Until then I don't want any fool shooting himself or one of our own men by accident." He took the time to inspect every single rifle, so Uno realized that clumsy soldiers had already lost some battles for this officer.

"It's nearly sundown," said Lieutenant De Soto. "We are to receive some food – it ought to be here in a short while – and some other supplies. They will be coming on the trail we just followed, but don't raise the alarm if you hear men approaching from that direction. I will post a sentry to watch for them. Sergeant Díaz will take the first watch at the riverbank, I will take the second, Díaz third, and I again the fourth, if it takes that long for the attack force to get here. Sergeant Díaz, call out your men and put them into position."

Sergeant Díaz rose. "Navarro, Escobar, Ramírez, Sandoval –" He told off the names of nine men.

Uno and Lolo scrambled to their feet.

"Fall in!"

The line of men on the heels of Sergeant Díaz started off into the jungle. Uno and Lolo brought up the rear.

"Damn," grunted Lolo, "I hate to go to war on an empty stomach!"

They halted on the lip of the low bank that overhung the river. In the failing light the surface of the water was like a dull mirror against the shadowy jungle that rose like walls on each side of the sluggish current. The strip of sky above the river – the only sky they could see – was the same color as the river, a blue-gray shading into green in the west. The river looked hard and impenetrable, while the sky had a transparent quality. Uno thought if a person or a bird could fly high enough into it he would find himself flying through blue air. He described this thought to Lolo as they waited for Sergeant Díaz to assign positions to them.

Lolo grunted. "Forget the sky. It's empty. But there may be loyalists on the other side of the river."

Uno nodded. Why did Lolo seem to know so much about war and being a soldier? He seemed to know things before they were taught. Lolo was probably going to be a great hero, while he, Uno, would trip over his own feet and shoot himself, or die of snakebite.

There were a few sounds they could hear, and Uno catalogued them. Soft thumps and clicks off to the right were the sounds of Sergeant Díaz positioning the other men. That rippling sound was the river as it spilled over fallen tree trunks at the water's edge. The squawking and flapping from across the river came from a huge dead tree where a large flock of egrets was settling in for the night. The big white birds seemed almost luminous in the twilight. Uno wished he were an egret. How nice it must be to belong to a race of beings who never went to war.

Sergeant Díaz appeared out of the darkness. "You two," he grunted, jabbing them with his rifle barrel. "Down here."

Uno and Lolo scrambled to their feet and stumbled through the darkness after him. There were no lights anywhere, and Uno was sweating for fear of stepping on a snake. He felt vines lash his face and the thorns of a chichicaste bush rake his skin; his feet slipped in the mud underfoot.

In a few moments Díaz halted. Uno could make out his square bulk silhouetted against the leaden surface of the river just beyond.

"Here. You will take cover behind this log. You will be able to see both straight across the river and also upriver. If anyone moves over there pass a signal back to me. If you hear voices, a sound like someone moving around or a boat on the river, let me know – but be quiet about it. *Don't* yell. *Don't* shoot. The loyalists may attempt to come downriver to keep us from crossing here tomorrow. Be on the alert for the sound of paddles."

Lolo squinted across the glassy water where one star in the eastern sky was now reflected. "Will they attack us from across the river?"

"Probably not. But they may have scouts out because they will expect us to attack them. They will know we have to try to retake San Ildefonso. They will try to stop us."

Uno and Lolo sank down to the boggy ground behind the log. Their rifles made the only straight lines they could see, with the butts resting beside them and the barrels stark against the faintly gleaming river.

Sergeant Díaz turned to go. "I'll be about five or six meters to the right of you. I can hear you – if you see anything, signal me. Don't talk louder than we are talking now. Don't talk at all unless you have to. And don't go to sleep. God help you if you go to sleep. I'll kill you myself if I come back and find you asleep." He turned and they heard him moving away, although by now it was so dark they could see nothing.

When Sergeant Díaz was gone Uno twisted first to the left and then to the right. Behind them and to the left was the black wall of the jungle, ahead and somewhat to the left the open slash of the river. To the right, jungle again. He figured he and Lolo were at the farthest left position facing the river; the other seven men and Sergeant Díaz were in positions stretching some distance down the riverbank to their right. He was grateful for the faint glimmer of light reflected by the river; it was the only break in the intense darkness of the night, and it gave him at least a slight sense of direction and place.

For several minutes they simply sat there. Mosquitoes whined in clouds around them, and they alternately fought and cursed as they felt the stings on face, neck, hands. The river was very quiet, but now and then some nocturnal animal made a faint sound along the margins. Once a faint cry, quickly silenced, scraped through the darkness.

"Jaguar," said Uno. "Caught something. At least *he's* eating."

"Watch out. Sergeant Díaz –"

"Here he comes," cut in Uno, hoping that the bulky shape

he could barely make out behind Lolo was indeed Díaz.

"Shut up!" snapped the sergeant. "I could hear you clear over to my position. Here – eat these."

Their hands snapped out, and each felt a couple of cold burritos laid in them. Silenced, they fell to stuffing food into their mouths, and chewing, swallowing, as if they were afraid the food would be snatched away from them.

"Have you heard anything?" asked Sergeant Díaz.

Uno gulped. "Only a jaguar. Nothing else."

"I heard the jaguar. I mean men – boats."

"Nothing, Sergeant."

"Keep awake. And alive. Remember – signal. Don't shoot." They did not see him go. In the darkness they could see nothing; one moment he was there and the next he was gone.

Lolo was licking his fingers. "I feel better now, except I'd like to sleep."

"Better not."

"No. So then – I wish we could get on with the war."

"You're in a hurry to die?" Uno asked.

"Why not? Little by little, or all at once. We'll get malaria if we sit here all night. Why not kill some loyalists to pass the time?"

But an hour or more passed and the war seemed suspended in the thick black air. Uno had a feeling the war was like a cloud or a vapor seeping through the forest around them and at some point it would condense, like rain, and start to fall. He started to describe this thought to Lolo when Lolo reached out a hand to touch his arm. It was their signal for silence.

Instantly Uno gave all his attention to listening. At first he could not discover what Lolo had heard, but then he picked it up too. It was the faintest tick of one drop of water falling on more water –

"Boat," breathed Lolo.

They leaned forward. In the darkness even the river was hard to see now. Only in the center of the current where the stars were mirrored was it possible to see anything; the banks were impenetrable.

Then, against the stars mirrored in the water, Uno began to see a dark shape. It was large, irregular, moving with the current.

"Sergeant," he whispered. "Boat!"

He rocked forward on his knees and leaned as far out over the log as he could without making any sound.

"No – two, three boats," said Lolo softly.

They felt Díaz as he moved closer to them, smelled his tobacco and sweat. "Quiet," whispered Díaz. "Don't shoot till I do. Safeties off." Then he was gone.

Uno's hand moved forward to release the safety on his rifle. He knew Lolo was doing the same. He wanted to yell out – ask somebody what he should do – but it was too late for that –

On the black mirror of the water they now clearly saw the three boats. They were not canoes – too large – and each carried several men. Utterly silent, they were drifting with the current, using paddles only to correct their position and hold away from the banks.

The first boat came abreast of them and moved on, then the second. When the third boat was just passing them Uno felt a chill tingle in his right hand. "When – ?" he mouthed.

"Wait –" Lolo barely breathed.

Then out of the night down the right bank of the river an explosion of noise broke the silence.

"Fire!"

Uno's arm snapped up. Without a split second's hesitation he aimed and fired at the black shapes in the third boat. They were not men – they were shapes – black shapes – he fired – fired – fired –

The noise was terrible. Men in the river screamed – Uno had never heard such screams –

The water turned molten in the flashes from the guns – somebody threw up some kind of flare that lit the awful scene –

Men fell into the water and struggled. Men on the bank shot at them. One by one the men in the water sank – and the boats floated on down the river.

As the flares died out Uno could see that the boats were all empty.

Most of the bodies floated away too, all but one which came to rest in the shallows a few feet away from the log behind which Uno and Lolo crouched.

Uno stared silently out over the black river. I did it, he told himself. I did it. I am one of them. I did it –

All night long the body lay there. When, two hours or so after the gun battle, Sergeant Díaz tapped them on the shoulder and led them back to the clearing, while the second squad took over the watch, they could still see the man's legs thrust out into the shallows. Even though Uno knew the loyalist had to be dead, he kept thinking that the man was going to regain consciousness and rise up with a terrible shout and come up the bank and shoot them. All the bodies of the other slain loyalists had floated downriver except this one. There had to be a reason.

"He's not dead," muttered Uno as they followed Díaz back to the clearing. "He's pretending. He's going to find some way to kill us –"

"You mean the man there in the water? He's dead," said Lolo.

"He's probably got a gun hid – he'll wait till we're asleep –"

"He's dead," said Lolo. "I shot him."

"He's going to –"

"And Sergeant Díaz went down and cut his throat. I heard him."

Uno froze in the darkness, and the soldier behind walked into him. Forced to move, Uno stumbled forward. Cut, he said to himself. Of course. With a machete. Like you cut cane –

At the clearing they were offered the second squad's vacated hammocks, together with cups of water and a few pieces of broken, dry tortillas. Ignacio had gone on watch with the second squad; there was only time for a brief glance before he disappeared into the darkness with the others.

Uno crawled into his hammock, but, still unable to thrust the memory of the dead soldier away from him, said at last, "All right – he's dead. Yes, I know."

Lolo's hammock creaked as he sank into it. "It was a good

shot," he said. "I got him just as he reached the bank. I heard his Uzi hit the water. Díaz will probably try to find it in the morning. An Uzi is valuable."

"And he'll give you a medal."

Lolo grunted. He was trying to stretch his single thin blanket around his shoulders to keep the damp chill out. "No medals," he muttered. "Not in this war. Go to sleep."

And in a few moments Uno realized that Lolo was asleep. Relaxed, comfortable, asleep.

But he lay for another hour wishing he too could sleep and feeling the tortillas in his belly sloshing around in the water he had drunk, like the body of the dead loyalist sloshing in the river. He listened to Lolo's gentle breathing only an arm's length away and thought, Lolo is a soldier. He's a good soldier. I fired my gun – this time I really did – but I probably didn't hit anybody. Lolo does it right. He and Nacio and the others are learning and doing it all right. But I'm probably as useless as Esteban said the baby was. Even Mendoza – Díaz – can't make a good soldier out of me –

Then he remembered the time – only five days ago? – when he had charged yelling up the ridge and "captured" it.

At that moment he had had some faint flash of understanding. He had known then – for just a second or two – that there were things a good soldier would do for his friends that he wouldn't do for himself. Maybe that's what *makes* a good soldier, he thought. I wish I could talk to Mendoza about this. I wish I could talk to Lolo about it.

DAY EIGHT

Before daybreak he woke again. He heard whispering voices and quickly realized they belonged to Díaz and the lieutenant. He strained to hear and decided they were arguing about something.

"— gave our position away —"

"No. They wouldn't have had time to radio —"

"Noise. Could have heard our guns a mile or more. We've got to fall back —" That was Lieutenant De Soto. Uno had the impression that De Soto was less experienced than Díaz, even if he was an officer.

Then Díaz spoke again. "We can't fall back. Mendoza and the rest of the main force will be here by dawn and will cross the river to launch the attack against San Ildefonso. We have to hold."

"We'll be wiped out."

"We've seen nothing since the boats. And it's only an hour till dawn. We have to hold." Díaz's voice was unyielding.

The conversation either ended then, or else they moved off. Uno could not tell, but he could not go to sleep again either. Dawn, he told himself. The rest of the army — all of it, I guess – will be here and there will be a big battle. He remembered seeing the SAMs, the small rocket launchers, one of which had been carried on the patrol but never fired. Juan had even said that the revolutionaries had some helicopters – gun ships. Perhaps they too would be used in this battle for San Ildefonso.

He wondered what it would be like to fight in a big battle. It must be very different from the patrol. He thought of the men, guns, helicopters massing right now in the secret green tunnels of the jungle and how in an hour they would burst out of those hiding places to throw themselves at the enemy.

And when it starts – what about me? I shot last night, but it was dark. Everybody was shooting. I couldn't see anything. It was not like shooting *at* someone. A man. They were just shadows. Shapes. But it will be daylight soon. Can I –

But then his stomach began to turn sour and cramped, and he knew he must not think too much about the battle. So for a few moments he thought about the city of San Ildefonso and the Easter celebration. I wish I could see it all again, he thought. I wish we could all be young and together again and it could be Easter forever. Some day, when I am old, I would like to go there again, at Easter, and see the procession, and the Christ in Bondage, the cathedral. But not the rooster . . .

He had just decided to crawl out of his hammock and go wake up Lolo and talk to him when a whispered signal passed around the clearing. The twenty men squirmed, scratched, crept out of their blankets like animals poked with sticks to rout them out of their dens.

There was only water to drink – no coffee – but one of

the men off watch was directed by Sergeant Díaz to distribute some cold beans and tortillas. Ignacio was on watch again, but Uno and Lolo stood together while they gulped down their food. Uno always felt so much better with food in his belly and Lolo standing nearby.

They were told to care for private needs by going into the jungle – not too far – and to roll mess kits up inside blankets and pack other supplies as if to move out. Uno noticed that Lieutenant De Soto seemed somewhat agitated. Díaz was silent, as usual, but even so, Uno sensed or smelled something different about him. When he got a chance, he tried to probe Díaz for information.

"Sergeant Díaz, what will your orders be for today?"

Díaz glanced up in surprise. He evidently hadn't thought Uno soldier enough to try to get his thoughts arranged for whatever was to come.

"We are to hold here. The main force is moving up and will cross the river today to attack San Ildefonso. But we have already picked up radio signals, and we know the loyalists will try to stop us from crossing the river."

Uno nodded. "What if the loyalists attack us first?"

Díaz smiled faintly. "Ah, the little soldier is improving. He tries to think of what will happen so he will be ready. Yes – they may well attack before Mendoza gets here. Just to get us out of the way, like you swat a mosquito. But we are not mosquitoes to be swatted. We will hold."

Uno went back to Lolo and Ignacio, who had returned from watch, and found them loading ammunition clips into their AK-47s, with extra clips thrust under their belts.

Lolo handed Uno two clips. "Sergeant Díaz says be careful. This is all the ammunition we've got till the rest of the army gets here. Two clips per man."

"How the hell can we –"

"Shut up. Fire single shots, not automatic. And aim carefully. *Aim.*"

Uno loaded his gun in silence. Lolo knew, then. Lolo knew he hadn't shot anybody on the patrol, and maybe not last night either. How does Lolo know things about me and I don't know things about him? he wondered. But then, maybe I do . . . I know Lolo would never hurt a person except this way, in a war. And I know – I know he would never give up and run and leave his friends behind – he was thinking about the rooster again – and I know that he and Ignacio will be great men some day.

This last thought surprised him. It had come like one of those flashes of lightning that suddenly light up the jungle so that every leaf is revealed and then as suddenly disappear. But all the same he knew it.

A few minutes later Díaz appeared. The dawn was only minutes away. The birds had already begun their morning ceremonies and their noise covered any the soldiers might inadvertently make. Even so, Díaz signaled for quiet.

He gathered them close and gave his instructions. "Each one of you will be assigned a post. You are to be absolutely silent unless we are attacked. If the loyalists attempt to break across the river we must stop them. Make every bullet count. Aim carefully, take your time. Mendoza and the other units will be here in a very short time. They *must* cross the river. If they can cross the river they can take San Ildefonso. If they cannot take San Ildefonso the battle will be lost. Every man must give his best."

"And if they attack us before the others get here?" This from Lolo.

"Don't return their fire until I give the signal. Don't shoot trees and bushes – they are not our enemies. When it's time to fire, I will give the signal." Díaz was, as always, threatening, but today Uno thought he had something else in his face. Uno wondered if it might be the expression of a soldier who goes into battle not because he knows he will win but because he is a soldier.

Then, one by one, Díaz and De Soto led the men to their posts.

Uno and Lolo drew the same spot they had been in the night before and again were at the far left end of the concealed line of men. Nacio was out of sight, somewhere toward the far right end of the line.

As Uno and Lolo settled behind the big log, Uno found he could not look down at the spot where the loyalist soldier had fallen at the edge of the water. He looked hastily around, checked his gun, looked up as a bird flew overhead.

"He's gone," said Lolo.

Uno jerked around.

"He's gone. The body is gone. River probably washed it away."

Uno nodded weakly. I was right, he thought. Lolo does know what I'm thinking.

"When – I wonder – how soon will the rest get here?" he

whispered, trying to see back into the jungle behind them.

"Not long, I guess. Díaz will –"

There was absolutely no warning.

One moment the jungle was silent and the brown river pulsing quietly a few feet away, and the next moment machine-gun fire burst out of the jungle across the river.

It was so sudden they simply sat there frozen. Then Uno looked at Díaz – he could barely see him – but Díaz made no signal. After a second, Uno realized Díaz must be waiting for the firing to end. Short on ammunition, the revolutionaries could not respond to the raking fire from across the river; they would have to wait till the loyalists charged – if they did – so each of them could use his scant supply of bullets on individual targets.

The firing stopped. The jungle was absolutely silent. Not a bird chirped; the monkeys had vanished. Uno could feel his heart pounding in his chest, hear his own breathing. He waited for the signal to return fire, but no signal came.

The silence lasted perhaps a minute. Then the firing began again from across the river. This time there was a systematic plowing of bullets up and down the bank. It made Uno think of the times he had watched the great diesel tractors of the estates in the cane fields and how the plows they pulled raked under all leaves, stalks, twigs. The riverbank began to look chewed.

But not one revolutionary had fired his rifle. Why didn't Díaz signal? Was he wounded? Uno wondered desperately. Was he dead?

Then it came again. This time the burst of fire lasted several minutes. Uno knew that although Díaz had positioned the men to have the best possible cover, there was too much firepower. Sooner or later someone would be hit.

Just as the firing ceased, he heard a faint cry off to the right. It was smothered instantly.

Then he heard Díaz say softly, "Get ready." A moment later the loyalists burst through the green wall of jungle on the opposite side of the river. They were moving fast. They carried rifles and Uzis, and several men stumbled under the burden of inflated rubber boats. In seconds they had the boats in the water and had scrambled through the shallows to clamber into them. Paddles bit into the current. Uno counted two – seven – nine boats – each boat loaded with several men. They were far outnumbered.

"Wait," signaled Díaz.

"But – ?" Uno felt his hands trembling on the rifle stock. Sweat was streaking down his face, his back.

"Wait," said Lolo.

The boats had reached midriver.

"Fire!"

Uno lunged upward and flung himself belly-down over the log. His rifle was up. There. Chest of a loyalist soldier. Pull the trigger. Chest of another. Pull the trigger. Head – no, I'll miss – stomach – chest – pull the trigger. He had no idea if he was hitting the targets. Everything was a screaming blur –

It went on –

To the right he heard a new sound. Chunk! Chunk! Chunk!

"Rocket launcher!" shouted Lolo.

"Where's Mendoza?" screamed Uno. "We can't hold –"

Some of the boats had sunk, some were nearly across. Now Uno could see the faces of the loyalists. He ripped out his empty clip and slammed in the full one, took aim. Once again he had no idea if he was hitting anyone. He just kept firing because he had to.

Then he heard a new sound. From behind them came a steady roar and a beating, exploding sound. Mendoza's force broke through the jungle cover, firing over their heads. Uno stopped shooting, crouched beside the log as streams of men pounded past him down to the river.

The moment they had gone past, Díaz raised them with a hand signal. "Charge!"

Now it was time. Uno got to his feet, fell over the log, crashed down the bank.

But he could not see who to shoot. Revolutionaries were in front of him. He raised his gun barrel and a loyalist soldier appeared on the opposite bank. He shot him.

Beside him Lolo was doing the same thing.

It went on. It went on. Uno was crying, and his feet were sliding in water – no, it was blood –

Suddenly someone turned from in front of them and ran back up the bank where they had been hidden. It was Whistler. He was screaming. He threw down his rifle and ran screaming into the forest.

Now the revolutionary troops were into the river, which was thick and clotted with bodies floating away. To his right Díaz plunged into the river, signaling them to follow. Uno plowed ahead as he hit the water, but he grabbed a quick look back and saw Lolo close behind. Lolo raised his rifle to club a loyalist over the head. He sank beneath the water, and Lolo lunged ahead.

The water was chest-deep, brown, and opaque. Uno felt

a stab of fear as its weight and power seized him and the muddy, oozy bottom sucked at his feet. He held his rifle high and half swam, half waded. The instant the water became shallower he lowered his rifle to take aim and resumed fire.

On the opposite bank they plunged into jungle almost as thick as the river water. On all sides, ahead and behind, Uno saw revolutionaries pounding forward. The front ranks were still firing, but the men in Uno's area held off to keep from shooting their own troops.

"Halt! Hold!" Díaz's voice cracked through the trees.

Uno staggered to a blind stop, gasping for breath. Water was streaming from him and green slimy weeds were tangled around his feet.

"*Bajense!* Down!"

They sank silently to the jungle floor. Uno crouched beside a tangle of tree roots. He tried to be quiet, catch his breath, guess what was going on. The men around him now were strangers – he had lost sight of Lolo and Ignacio and the rest of his own squad. Where were they? He leaned forward, then sideways, spread the leaves with his gun barrel, but could see no one he recognized. Fear slashed through him as he searched the faces of the three or four men he could see. He wanted to ask frantic questions – What's happening? Where's Díaz? What are we going to do? But their set faces silenced him. Shaking, he bit down on his lip so he wouldn't yell out and tried to remember their training. Hold on, he told himself. Hold on. Don't panic. Don't run. Remember Whistler.

Perhaps five minutes passed. Then Uno sensed a ripple of some kind approaching down the line of men. Presently a team of men appeared, working their way from man to man.

They were heavily laden – ammunition. They handed each man six clips.

Uno took out his empty clip, put in a full one, stuck the other five into his belt.

"Wait for the signal," said one of the ammunition carriers. "You will hear the whistle. We will advance slowly, moving straight ahead. If we don't run into loyalists we are to continue till we take the ridge overlooking San Ildefonso. It's about ten kilometers. We will halt there and get ready for an attack." Then the ammunition carriers were gone and the jungle fell silent. This time the other soldiers relaxed a little. One went behind a clump of ferns to relieve himself; the smell was pungent, almost animal, in the heavy air.

It wouldn't be so bad, thought Uno, if I could see Lolo. If I could just *see* him –

Then the whistle sounded. They got to their feet and began the advance, slowly, tree by tree, bush by bush, in the dense shadowy jungle.

He had no machete and had to detour around the worst thickets. Sometimes he drew ahead; sometimes he fell behind, and that frightened him the most. For some reason he could not fathom it seemed much worse to be left behind in the silent forest than to be out at the breast of the line, where he could take a loyalist bullet at any moment. But then nothing made sense anymore.

They advanced for two, maybe three, hours, crossing only two overgrown tracks that led through the jungle, perhaps to abandoned lumber camps. At last the ground under their feet began to rise, sloping upward toward some crest they could not see, and there was a gradual change in the jungle. After they traversed another half kilometer, climbing steadily, the trees thinned and the air became drier. Walking was much easier, and Uno could see far enough to locate ten or twenty men on each side of him. He knew that the line, though, was much longer and that there were waves of men ahead and possibly behind him too.

Suddenly the sky beyond the trees began to lighten. The undergrowth thinned and a horizon appeared – the crest of the low ridge above San Ildefonso. Uno remembered the ridge from the time he had been here as a child. The city's outermost streets were not more than half a kilometer from where they now stood.

"Halt." The command passed, and they sank to their knees, grateful for dry ground underneath and for the faint breeze lifting up out of the valley around San Ildefonso.

Uno found a place to sit where he could see a fair amount of the back side of the ridge and the ragged line of men stretched along just beneath the crest. The revolutionaries sat in clusters, alert but relaxed. Uno began to pick out officers, sergeants, corporals, moving here and there, but still no one that he knew. A few men had been wounded crossing the river; bandages were brought out now and some treatment given.

Then a team of men appeared bearing canteens of water and baskets from which they handed each man a couple of tortillas. Another man followed with a metal bucket and a spoon; he served each man a spoonful of beans on his tortillas. Uno felt his stomach grind at the sight of food. When his turn came he was hard-pressed to wait quietly in his place, but when he looked at the iron faces of the men around him, he knew he would not move. Whistler, he reminded himself, ran away from enemy fire. I won't bolt for a drink of water and something to eat.

When they received their food, they ate it in silence and as fast as possible, choking one bite down after another.

They rested for perhaps half an hour. While he sat there, Uno tried to calculate the time. The main force had been expected to arrive at the river at dawn. Counting the time it had taken for the attack at the river and the crossing, the short pause there, and maybe three hours or more for them to come this far through the jungle, it must be now nearly eleven o'clock in the morning. Knowing what time it must be made him feel a little better, but he knew that he was only counting up time to take his mind off his worst concerns – Lolo and Ignacio.

He had not seen Lolo since they crossed the river and had not even seen Nacio then. He knew that some revolutionaries had been hit during the crossing. Was Lolo one of them? Nacio? He wondered if there were the slightest possibility of trying to find them.

Moving very slowly – telegraphing his intentions, as Mendoza had told him to do around these hair-trigger fighters – he got to his feet. He waited a moment to see if anyone would challenge him. No one did. He looked around carefully, spotted a sergeant, made sure the soldiers around him grasped his direction, and then moved quietly toward him.

The sergeant was staring silently down the slope into the forest.

"Sir . . ."

The sergeant turned slowly, gave him a long look. Finally he said, "You don't say 'sir' to a sergeant. I am Sergeant Cardoza. What do you want? Be quick about it and get back to your place."

"Yes, sir! No, sir! I mean – is it possible to ask – I am worried about – my friend. I haven't seen him since we crossed the river –"

Sergeant Cardoza looked at him, and Uno thought he had a very tired look. Almost as if he himself were wounded, though Uno could see no blood or bandages on him. Finally the sergeant spoke. "You are . . . a *cuque* – a new recruit?"

"Yes – sir. Yes. And my friend – the one I can't see now – we came from the same village – the same day, a few days ago. He is . . . my oldest friend. And there is also – my cousin. We all three came together. And two of us were together when we crossed the river, but now –"

Sergeant Cardoza nodded tiredly. "Yes. I see. But I cannot allow you to go searching up and down the lines now. We are preparing to advance on San Ildefonso as soon as our gun ships arrive. But I can tell you this – I do not believe any men were lost" – he emphasized the word "lost," and Uno knew he meant "killed" – "crossing the river, though a few were wounded. It is most probable that you all simply got separated, and they are somewhere here on the ridge. But, for now, you must keep your mind on the battle. We will attack San Ildefonso very soon."

Uno nodded crisply and thanked the sergeant, who had, after all, been kind enough to at least talk to him. Then he turned and made his way back to his place in the line. So, he told himself, they are probably all right, probably here some-place. God, take care of them –

He had barely gotten back and sat down when all up and

down the line there was a sudden electric stir. Men raised their heads to search the sky, and Uno could not tell if they were relieved or afraid. Then out of the heat haze hanging back over the lowlands and the river came a powerful throbbing sound. Quickly several black dots appeared in the sky and on closer approach were revealed to be large helicopters. There were six of them, and they swept in from behind the revolutionaries, low over the ridge. By the cheers and waves of the men about him, Uno knew they belonged to the revolution. At the moment of their passing the noise of their engines and rotors, and the down draft of air, were so overpowering Uno thought they would be swept off the ridge. Then the gun ships had passed over, and almost instantly he heard the heavy chunk! chunk! chunk! of shells hitting the ground. They were so close to the city, though hidden behind the ridge, that Uno thought he could tell the difference in sound when a shell struck a wooden house or a brick building and the shattering of glass, the screech of torn metal.

The whistle blew.

Uno sprang to his feet, one man in the ragged line of green uniforms that now surged forward, crested the ridge, and rushed down on the other side.

Uno ran elbow to elbow with the rest of them, dodging the low walls of outlying gardens and the rubble of the first small houses smashed by the artillery fire from the gun ships. No one among the troops was shooting yet, so he carried his rifle up at high ready waiting to follow the lead of others.

In a matter of minutes their steady onrushing pace brought them onto paved streets. Ahead of them, fleeing like cattle from a hungry jaguar, a few civilians raced in the other direction. Men and women carried children, and all of them stared back with faces convulsed with fear at the green tide of revolutionaries with rifles, small arms, rocket launchers.

But the charge slowed down quickly now. Sergeants and corporals and officers picked off squads to search buildings as they advanced. There was a sound of rifle fire from time to time – and here and there fires broke out, started by artillery shells striking cars with tanks full of gasoline or wooden buildings.

The greasy smoke made Uno sick, but it also was an excuse for the tears he felt sliding down his cheeks. It's just the smoke, he told himself, as he ran, and he tried not to see a cat hiding under a wrecked house, a child's schoolbooks scattered in the street.

Suddenly, ahead of him, he saw Sergeant Cardoza. The sergeant halted, turned, jabbed his rifle at Uno. "Ramírez, over here! Silva – Morales – Gomez – search this house!"

The sergeant kicked open the wrought iron gate set in a high plastered wall, and Uno and the others plunged after him.

It was like stepping through a magic barrier and leaving the war behind. The sound of shots was not so loud or the stink of smoke and blood so strong.

But they were still soldiers. They searched the empty courtyard, found nothing but a couple of chairs, some ornate jars of plants, and the lower rooms. Finding no one, they charged up the outdoor staircase. In spite of the rifle in his hands, Uno had a crazy feeling that at any moment the owner of the house would leap out at them and order them out of his house.

But the house was empty. The large rooms, expensively furnished, showed the haste with which the occupants had left – clothing dropped, food spilled on a table – there was even some money on the floor in one of the bedrooms. Uno saw it but did not touch it. He still felt the owner would see – and accuse him.

When they were back out on the street, Uno looked around. And he suddenly realized that they were now moving into the square facing the cathedral.

He stared up at the face of the old church and his heart stopped. Shell after shell must have struck it, gaping holes were everywhere in the ornate plaster façade. The statues of the gentle saints looked like dead bodies hanging up there, and one of the bell towers was half blown away. Uno thought it looked like a great screaming mouth –

"Forward! Into the church –"

They crossed the square at a flat-out run. Bullets were raking across the square and men were going down. Ahead of Uno a soldier stumbled as blood exploded from his thigh.

It was Juan. Without missing a step, Uno reached down and grabbed Juan's arm and dragged him on across the square and up the cathedral steps, through the great carved doors, out of the deadly, withering gunfire. It took only a second to prop him against the foot of a huge pillar – their eyes met – and then Uno turned to follow Sergeant Cardoza.

"Hold! We'll have to search for snipers –"

For one moment all of them halted. The dozen or more revolutionaries stood rigid, silent, raking their eyes around at the nave of the cathedral that arched over them like a hollow shell of stone and the battered, shell-pocked walls. Here inside the great stone building, it was a little quieter, and the tall pillars along the aisles stood up like ancient trees, but harsh bright sunlight slashed through gaping holes in the roof and in the stained-glass windows. The light fell over the floor where broken chairs lay overturned and splintered, and papers, books, colored vestments were strewn about.

Sergeant Cardoza started forward toward the altar, signaling men to search the aisles and chapels. Uno moved forward slowly, feeling the rubble of dust and plaster and broken glass underfoot. In the dazzle of dusky corners and glaring beams of light it was hard to see anything clearly.

He halted near the altar rail. Off to his left Sergeant Cardoza had located a priest, who had been kneeling at the side of the altar, and the squad paused, guns at the ready as they waited for further signals from Cardoza.

Uno stared around him. This was the church of that happy Easter. These were the pillars, the great colored windows, the paintings of saints and miracles from long ago.

Then he remembered the Christ. Yes, there it was, off to his right.

Still holding his gun at the ready, he moved slowly toward it and stood at last at its feet, looking up.

This was the Christ in Bondage that his parents had brought him to see – the one beside which the rooster had been penned. "And the rooster was to remind us that all of us can fail," he told himself now, "like Whistler."

He looked up at the statue's face. It was a mask of sorrow, and over the whole figure lay a death-white shroud of plaster dust. A few days ago he had dreamed of going back to that Eastertime when he and his family had been happy. And now, he thought, I am here – and it is war – and the Christ is in bondage still.

But – he looked around – the rooster is gone. I would like to tell that rooster something, he thought. I would like to say, "Hey, rooster, I didn't run. Whistler ran away. But *I* didn't!"

There was a shout behind them – Juan's voice, he realized. They whirled. A loyalist soldier, concealed somewhere, had sprung up, firing an Uzi, and the bullets went over them like a spray of boiling water –

Uno raised his gun to return fire.

Instantly more revolutionaries poured into the church, closing in on the sniper.

Uno felt something strike him on the shoulder – hard – hard – and at the same time saw Sergeant Díaz far up the aisle, running toward him –

And then it all vanished –

When he opened his eyes he was lying in the jungle. Looking up he saw the canopy of ceiba trees against a burning blue sky, and something about the color of the sky made him think, It's almost evening. What happened to the rest of the day?

He heard some voices around him, but he was very tired. Too tired to look. There was a dull, deep pain in his shoulder and down through his chest, and he sensed that his left arm was bound tightly against him.

Then, above him, framed in the canopy of trees, he saw a face. Nacio.

"Well, soldier. It's time you woke up." Nacio looked mad, but somehow Uno did not think he was really mad. He tried to turn his head. The trees all stood on their heads.

"Be still." Another face – Olivares.

If he couldn't get up, he could talk. "Where . . . what time . . . did we . . . ?"

Olivares bent to look at Uno's bandages. "We had to fall back. It's six o'clock. You managed to get yourself shot. Bullet broke your collarbone and tore up some of your shoulder."

Uno glared. Olivares acted as though he had got shot on purpose just to get out of the battle. "Did . . . we . . . ?"

Ignacio leaned over him. "Be quiet. No. We . . . did not capture San Ildefonso. We killed a damn lot of loyalists, but we didn't take San Ildefonso."

Uno closed his eyes. So the trees would get right-end-up. "Then . . . we lost."

"Yes. We lost."

He rested for a while, slept in snatches. He was aware that there were people around, but not many. He heard voices, the click of rifles being cleaned, a few arguments. He knew they were still in the jungle and that he was lying on the ground, although there seemed to be a blanket under him now.

He wished the dizziness and stupor would go away because there were things he wanted to think about – important things. Like the mercenaries – everyone had been so excited about them, but he had never seen them, and it was clear that they had not helped win the battle for San Ildefonso. Then there were Choya and his men who helped carry the captured rifles and ammunition back to the fortress. Choya could have been there fighting with us, he thought, but he was probably off somewhere in the jungle where it was safe, counting the money he makes off both sides. And as badly as Uno had come to hate the loyalists, he realized now that he hated Choya more. Choya was like a jaguar that attacks a child already weak from starvation. That thought reminded him of the girl, Magdalena, and tiny Manolete. He wondered if he would ever see them again. He hoped he would. He could still see the baby's grave and curious expression as he lay peacefully in Uno's arms and examined the world in which he had now to live.

Suddenly a wave of anguish broke over Uno. Mendoza said we would make a good world for you, Manolete! I believed him. Yes — at last I believed him. And we tried! We tried! *I* tried —

It was nearly dark when he woke again and realized that his head was clear. He was lying in another makeshift bed, but it was more comfortable than the first had been. He still could not see much, but he sensed that he was in a camp, because he could hear men's voices, the click and thump and rustle of soldiers going about the business of soldiers. A thin fragrance of coffee floated on the air, underscored by smoke from a wood fire.

Well. So I am alive, he thought. We lost the battle, but I am still alive. Díaz said we would be slapped like mosquitoes, but he was right — this mosquito is still alive.

Then he tried to roll over and sit up but immediately discovered that he was made of jelly that did not respond to commands. He lay for a few moments looking up and saw that the trees, while now right-end-up, were different from those he had seen earlier. While he had slept, the army must have moved deeper into the jungle.

There was a step and Nacio appeared. He carried a gun in one hand and some ammunition in the other as he bent over Uno. "You are awake again. I thought you planned to sleep forever."

Uno glared up at him. "Where are we? Help me sit up."

"We're sixteen kilometers beyond the river. Falling back toward the coast. We lost the battle. And you're not to sit up. You're still bleeding."

Uno digested some of this. Finally he asked, "Coast? What coast?"

"The east coast – above the mouth of the Santa María. Mendoza says there will be boats to take us off the beach, and they will put us ashore farther north. He says we will have to build another fortress – the loyalists bombed the old one – and we'll go underground for a few weeks, maybe months. We tore up a lot of loyalists, but they tore up a lot of us. Mendoza says the general wants us out of action so we can regroup. Get more training."

Nacio had sat down on the ground beside Uno, and Uno could see that he was quietly and curiously examining the gun in his hands.

"It's an Uzi," explained Nacio, seeing the direction of Uno's glance. "We captured a lot of them. They are from Israel. And they are fine, fine guns."

Uno stared at the gun. He was waiting for something. He

was waiting for Nacio to tell him something, but he realized now that Nacio was not going to speak voluntarily.

"Nacio — where's Lolo?"

There was a brief silence.

"Nacio — tell me — where's Lolo?" Uno turned slightly so that he could see Nacio better. His head swam, but, oddly, his vision was clear enough now to see the dark lines of Nacio's face. "*Tell* me, Nacio. Where is Lolo?"

But as the silence went forward, Uno clearly saw that there was something Nacio knew, but that it was better for him, Uno, not to know. Not now. Not yet . . .

Finally Nacio spoke. His voice was very low, so low that the wind passing overhead through the trees almost covered it.

"Lolo . . . was wounded. He was . . . evacuated by helicopter."

That was all he said.

Uno lay looking up at the green leaves of the trees, and he remembered the leaves he had gathered to lay on the graves at the lost village. But — *no! No green leaves for Lolo!* "He will be all right!" cried Uno suddenly. "Lolo — he will be *all right!*"

Nacio was still for a moment. Then he reached out and smoothed the rumpled bandages over Uno's shoulder. "Of course," he said.

"Of course," whispered Uno.

A moment went by, and then Uno, looking up past the trees, saw a spark of white — two — three — many, burning against the fading sky. A flight of white egrets were making their way to their home trees where they would roost for the night. Tomorrow they would fly again — fly and feed and make nests and go on being egrets and doing what egrets do — so long as no bullets, no rockets, no grenades tore them to bits or drove them out of the forest. Some of the egrets would be left even if others would die. The best they could hope for, Uno thought, was that a few of the birds stayed on, because the jungle needs egrets. *I* need egrets.

And now, at last, as he watched the egrets following their own course through the sky, and without anyone saying it, Uno realized that all of them — himself, Nacio, Lolo — had long since come to know that the fierce current of war that had swept them out of their village might well separate into many streams. And there had never been any guarantee that all of them would take the same stream.

Suddenly he was gripped by a sense of urgency. This army moved fast. He must talk to Nacio quickly, while he could. "Nacio — what is going to happen to us? To you and me. Now."

Nacio raised his head to look around at the camp, where men were already loading supplies into shell-scarred trucks. "They are getting ready to move out again. You will be put into one of the trucks with the other wounded."

"No — I mean — you and me — what will happen to us — now?"

Nacio nodded. He seemed tired, and yet Uno sensed that Nacio was beginning to hold some strength in reserve, inside him, to use as the war and the world made demands on him. "Yes," said Nacio. "I understand what it is you want to know. But I can't tell you very much. From now on — maybe forever — it will be like the battles. Like the patrol. We'll go where they send us."

"Go? Where? Where will they send us?"

Nacio hunched his shoulders and bent over till his lips were close to Uno's ear. "I am to – escape," he whispered very quietly.

"*Escape*? From the army? How?"

"Mendoza will arrange it."

"*Mendoza*? But he's –"

"He has decided that I must go north. He knows a man in the U.S. who will take me in – if I can get there – and send me to school. Mendoza wants me to be a doctor, like my father. He says the country must have doctors."

"Yes . . . doctors. Of course."

A brief silence fell again. Uno closed his eyes. Yes, Mendoza would know the country needs doctors, and, yes, Nacio would be a good one. It was Nacio who told Lolo about the antibiotics. And then out of a spasm of anguish he whispered suddenly, "Lolo. *Lolo*."

"He will be all right."

Uno knew that Nacio didn't know this any more than Uno did. But they had to say it, both of them. He hoped that at least some of it was true – that Nacio wasn't lying too much. "And . . ." he said slowly, at last, pronouncing each word carefully, as if someone were writing them down in a book, or carving them on stone, "and when he gets better, he will become an officer –"

"And – he will always go into battle wearing ballet slippers –"

"– and then we will win the war."

"Of course . . ."

"Of course."

They looked at each other, and Uno could see that Nacio's eyes were dry. So are mine, he thought. Soldiers don't cry. None of us soldiers cry. We just keep on fighting. Then: "What about the others? I thought I saw Whistler —"

Nacio nodded. "Yes, the big mean macho soldier who wanted to strangle babies couldn't stand up to the enemy in a fire fight. He threw down his gun and deserted."

"Juan — he was wounded when we were crossing the square," said Uno. "Where is he — did he — ?"

"Yes, he was wounded. But I heard that somebody pulled him into the church and saved him. His wound is not too bad. Mendoza said he would be sent to train with Godoy's army."

So . . . I did it, Uno thought. Nobody knows I saved Juan, nobody but me. But that's all right. I'm the only one who cares. I'm the only one who needs to know that I'm as good a soldier as Juan.

And finally he came to the last question. "What will happen to me?"

Nacio laid down his Uzi and leaned forward. His face was still, neither sad nor happy, but he reached out and his fingers just brushed the torn edges of Uno's bloody shirt sleeve. "You are to be sent home."

"*Home?*" He could not believe it. *Home?* He had never expected to see the village again.

Ignacio nodded as he tested the bindings on Uno's arm. "I talked to Mendoza before he left to get our units away from the river and out to the coast. He said that I should be sent to medical school because that was the best way I could serve our country. I am to cross the Mexican border and work my way — he meant 'walk,' of course — north to a town across the Río Grande from El Paso, Texas. Then I will write to Mendoza's friend in the U.S., and he will get me a student visa and I will go to school there. And Mendoza said you would be taken back to the mission by Choya – yes, Choya – to rest while your wound heals, and then Choya will see that you get back home. When you get there, I want you to tell my grandfather where I am and that I will write to him. But as for you – Mendoza says you must find some way to go back to school, to study. You must learn to read well, write, do mathematics. You will be contacted by the guerrillas, and they will give you a little money to help you with this. And Mendoza said you must talk to people. You must tell them that the country will be made better not just with guns and battles but with schools and hospitals and elections and laws. He said you must talk to people and convince them that all of us together can work for a better country. You must find a way to become a schoolteacher."

"Teacher? Me? But I'm – I'm a soldier! That's what they brought us here for – to be soldiers! What the hell was the use of it all – why did they take us from our village if we aren't going to be soldiers?" For one second a vivid memory of the money spilled on the floor of the house they searched – the money that he hadn't even touched – flashed through his mind. I should have grabbed it!

"Calm down," said Nacio. "You'll start bleeding again. And if we *had* stayed there – what would we have become? *Corteros* – *chicleros* – old men at twenty. Corpses at thirty. No – put that out of your mind, Uno. We left home to be soldiers, and that's what we will be. I'll be a doctor-soldier. You will be a teacher-soldier. Mendoza said he watched you at the village where the loyalists killed the people. He watched you with the girl, with the baby — even playing baseball. You work well with people. He said . . . he said in some ways you are the most important soldier of us all because you care about people. And he says that our country needs men who care about people, to serve."

"Serve . . ." said Uno slowly. "Serve . . ." He glanced up at Nacio. Nacio's face was closed as always, as in the packing sheds, but behind it Uno saw, like a glimpse of light beneath a closed door, that the word "serve" was the reason why he had not picked up the money. It was the answer to a puzzle, the answer to a question.

But it was a question that none of them had ever even asked until now. We came here, he thought, as prisoners, and now we are soldiers ready to serve. Something has happened to us, and it will take me all my life to understand it. I have become a soldier, and I will always be one, whether I am with the army or not. Yes, I'll go back the same as I went forward when Díaz led us across the river, into the city, into the cathedral. I'll go back because I'm a soldier now. From this day on, I will always be a soldier.

Then, aloud, he said regretfully, "But we lost . . . we lost . . ."

"We lost the battle, not the war," said Ignacio. "And anyway, our wars have been going on for a very long time —"

"Sure," Uno nodded slowly. "After all, you said this was the forty-third war."

"That's right."

"And so —" All at once Uno felt his breath fill his chest and his old strength begin to feed back into him. "And so all of us will go on learning what we have to learn and then"— he nodded slightly and Nacio nodded too, as if they had come to some mighty agreement even though it had never been discussed — "and then, whatever happens we will be ready — when the forty-fourth war comes —"

And he also knew that when he had to — when the forty-fourth war came — he would be able to kill the man with the big nose.

And, even without Lolo, that made him feel better.